This story is a v
incidents are fi
locations, or ev
to train artificia
No AI tools w
produce the artwork thereon.

ISBN: 978-1-998763-67-2
Second Edition

GET FREE

MARK ROBINSON

One.

Crashing through the bracken in a blur of night-tinged grey, Callie Ireson's bare footfalls pounded in time with the beating pulse in her ears. Inside her head, she was screaming. She had kept it all locked up just as the man had confined her in his cabin. Out there in the undergrowth, legs burning with the effort it took to whip between the trees, her choking lungs longed to let go.

Not yet. The low misty moon blinked down amongst the bare branches, reminding her of bones hung all around. Her zip-tied wrists, held up against her chest, kept in place what was left of her work shirt.

"Nobody knows you're out here." Those hollow words making the nape of her neck prickle, even now.

The man had done his homework. Callie

was single, had no kids, not much of a family left to speak of and shared little of her life with her new work colleagues.

She had been the perfect victim.

Shoulders swiping the trunks of two closely aligned trees, the impact pulled her out of her own aching head and back into the present. Or so she thought. All the careful planning in the world hadn't prepared him for what she was capable of.

A flash of the man's pale bloodied face as she stepped over him was encouragement enough for her to risk a quick glance behind her.

No one was pursuing her. The empty forest left in her wake helped to quell her sense of blind panic, but she wasn't stupid. The man in the cabin would come after her, sooner or later.

A fallen log tripped her. The shock made her call out, but her ruined feet kept her upright, though the jolt brought new pain to her already exhausted body. She wasn't going down like this. That's what she'd told herself over and over, again. It was her new mantra. As soon as the drugs had worn off and she had realized something wasn't right, Callie had promised herself this wouldn't be the end of her.

It was her thirtieth birthday in three days and she was determined to celebrate it.

Up ahead, the ground seemed to level out and the thicket of dense trees began to clear. In the gaps between them, Callie thought she saw a flash of light in the middle distance. Hope swelled in her chest and pushed her to keep on going. Blinking warm tears from her stinging eyes, she caught another trail of passing light. This time, accompanied by the sound of a car engine.

It was a road.

She was finally free!

Breathing out a cry of gratitude that had been held back, she willed her cramping leg muscles to deliver her to the roadside. The roadside where she could flag down a passing motorist who would save her life.

Pressing forward, no new lights lit the way, though she could now make out where the forest ended. There were no streetlights to guide her so she knew this wasn't a main road or motorway. To her right, a dark shape loomed up through the surrounding bushes. At first, she thought it was a small concrete building. But as she neared the road, Callie realized it was a bridge. And why she'd seen no more passing traffic as the ground had started to incline once more.

It was incredible. The whole time she'd been running alongside a canal towpath.

At the foot of the bushy embankment, Callie used her bound hands to pull herself, digging her broken nails into the hard earth as she hauled her way up onto the narrow, unlit tarmac road. Scrambling up from her hands and knees, Callie whirled left and right hoping to catch sight of another pair of approaching headlights.

Apart from her harsh breaths and wind rustling the forest, there was no other sound. Checking behind her, the gap where the canal bridge squatted, she was all alone.

Until…

At first, she thought the sound was all in her head. But it got louder, closer so that she clearly heard it for real. Then lights, bright lights, the approaching diesel engine, harsh and urgent against the quiet night.

Without thinking, Callie rushed to meet it, waving her bound hands as best she could. Help was finally here so she let go of everything she had been holding back until that point and screamed into the path of the approaching truck. Which began to slow. The interior bright, a stocky man high up behind the wheel, the look of absolute shock on his dark, unshaven face. She aimed for his side of the cab, spotting lights along the side revealing the shape of a tanker it was pulling.

A hiss of air brakes and rubble of rubber shuddering over tarmac.

Callie reached the cab door as the driver flung it open. "Help me, please!"

An arm outstretched, gripping hers, pulling her up into the cab. "Get in, you're alright now."

Once up the steps, he'd moved over so she could clamber inside. The driver, tattoos coloring his bare, hairy forearms, pulled back a curtain and gestured for her to sit down.

As she sat to rest, he fumbled with a nearby flask and offered it to her. "Coffee. It's black but it's sweet; it'll help with the shock."

Gratefully, she took it and gulped down the hot liquid. "Thank you."

Blinking back tears, the illuminated cluttered interior became a mess of bleeding colors. On the sat nav screen, a huge H dominated.

The driver saw it, too. "There's a hospital near here, you're going to be okay." Spotting her zip-tied wrists and reaching around for some pliers. "There." Not finished, he bent forward and pulled out a spare T-shirt for her to put on.

That's when the sobs took her. They wracked her body and she allowed them to come. Her dad had always told her not to keep her emotions in, to let everything go. And right there, that's what she did.

A crash against the back of the cab caught them both. It stilled her tears and the whole night around her. Instinctively, Callie thought it was the man who had taken her.

The confused eyebrows of her rescuer mirrored her own. "Stay put, okay?"

Callie wasn't planning on going anywhere without him, not tonight. Whatever it was, thudded against her back. If it wasn't her attacker, maybe it was something fighting to get out of the tanker.

"Is there something in there?" she asked him.

The driver shook his head, "Just waste

sludge," and took a torch, telling her he'd be right back.

Callie crawled forward to watch him leave, her eyes on the side mirror as his reflection jumped down from the cab and disappeared behind the trailer. There was a radio in front of her, the road ahead dark and empty outside the wide beam of the headlights. Each side of her, the woods were thick and dark, too. Torch light hitting the side mirror, pulled her eyes back. She heard a crash again. The light stopped moving then went away. Callie watched the driver aim it up toward the top of the tanker. A second or two passed before he jumped up and started climbing the steel ladders fixed to the side. Light bouncing around as he moved out of view.

From the side mirror, Callie went back to the woods, to the opposite mirror then to the windscreen, not taking anything for granted. Keeping her sights on her surroundings. The man who had taken her was still out there, somewhere. She may have left him unconscious when she got away, but she knew he wasn't dead. And, until then, that was the only time she would let herself fully relax.

Another thunking sound, louder this time and accompanied by what she thought was a muted splashing noise, drew her eyes back to the side mirror. Torch light bounced around from on top of the tanker before she heard a grating pop that hurt her ears. Metal clattered on the road. Callie saw a silver disc spin, wobble, and settle on the tarmac. A thump, a yell and ripping sounds rent the night air. Crashing down on the road, next to the silver disc, came a bloodied torch. Callie went to scream but no sound came out. Another scream, something close to a roar, and that's when her whole world came apart with a crack.

She looked on at the ruptured body of her rescuer, lying bloodied in the road.

Two.

Grace Wan hit the button for the electric windows, then cranked the volume. She was only two miles from home but the weariness of finishing a night shift at the hospital was usually enough to put her down.

But not tonight.

Although her body was nearing exhaustion, her mind was a hive of furious activity. It happened sometimes that, even despite the hour, her head would be wired and sleep would evade her until the sun began its ascent and birds tweeted their early morning calls. It would be the same tonight. Her thoughts lingering on the little girl she'd met, the one who came in close to death but would now be okay. Lucy had reminded her of her own little girl who was staying at her dad's this weekend which, in turn, reminded her of their empty house and leftovers in the fridge waiting for her to get home.

All these thoughts went when she rounded a bend and saw the tanker truck stationary in the center of the road. As she eased off the accelerator pedal, the headlights picked out a shape next to the tanker. Was that a…?

Stamping down on the brake, Grace ripped the steering wheel to the side to avoid the body lying in the road. As she pulled on the handbrake, the cab door was flung open. What she saw made Grace wrench open her own door and rush out to meet them.

The woman—mid to late twenties—ran toward her on bare legs, dark hair and baggy white T-shirt whipping out behind her. "You have to help me!"

Before she could get as far as the body, the half-naked woman was on her. Grace took hold of her and hugged her back tight. "What's going on?"

The sobs were too much to make sense of. Taking control, she urged the woman back to her car, all the time trying to settle her with reassuring words. Easing her down into the passenger seat, Grace—dressed in her nurses' scrubs—knelt down in the open door, still holding onto the girl's hands. "Are you hurt?"

In the soft glow from the interior light, the girl looked so lost. Her dark matted hair hung down to frame a face covered in scratches. Around her throat was an off-white piece of cloth with a knot on one side. It looked to her like a makeshift gag the girl had managed to push down. A too-big, baggy T-shirt enveloped her like a low-cut dress. Looking down at the hands holding hers, Grace noticed the wrists were red where they'd been tied together. Bare legs were cold with goose pimples. Those, too, were covered in scratches and cuts. And her feet were dirty. She'd really been through the mill.

"I'm okay." The girl simply shook her head in reply to the question, Grace had forgotten she'd asked. "And he didn't do any of this." Nodding at the body lying in the road then down at herself. Her next words caught in her throat. The girl scrunched up her expression as the tears slid down her face. "He was trying to help me."

Grace went for her phone. "I'm going to call the police, okay?"

The girl went to stop her; Grace had seen it before. All too often, the victims of abuse not wanting to report it to the authorities. So, she stood up, holding fast. There was nothing this girl could do or say to stop her doing her job.

"I've already called them."

Grace considered her. She'd heard that one before, too. Another delay tactic used by victims. Well, then, she'd just have to stick around until they came, the distant sounds of sirens in the air. Relief allowed her to breathe.

"Okay, then." Putting her phone away. "Sit tight, we're likely to be hanging around for a while before I can take you to the hospital." Crouching, Grace held out a hand and introduced herself.

Three.

"Knew I'd find you here."

Detective Sergeant Lucy Anderson almost jumped at the voice, fingers hovering at the coin slot in the vending machine. Detective Inspector Daniel Cross smiled down at her, that gap in his front teeth radiating calm.

"Knew I should've gone to the shop." It was cheaper than the vending machine but was at the other end of the yard. Despite the late hour, it would still be open. She pressed the last coin in and hit the faded buttons, watching the chocolate bar get pushed forward by the metal corkscrew. With a thud it dropped off the edge and into the drawer at her feet. "What's up?" Ready for business now that she had her sugar fix.

DI Cross nudged her aside as he pulled out a handful of change and shifted them into his palm. "A tanker truck driver's dead, his passenger survived. I'm told she's pretty shaken up."

Only ninety minutes left of her shift. Anderson checked her watch. She'd be lucky to make it home before dawn. "You're driving." Walking ahead of him toward the car park.

The clunk of the vending machine sounded behind her. "That's non-negotiable; you drive too slow." Came his reply.

It made her smile. She'd out-driven him in the tactical driving course they took three weeks ago. The only two Black detectives at the station in attendance and the only two to beat the county record. It burned him that she came out on top. He was so competitive but, at the same time, so laid back about it. She took every opportunity to rub his nose in it.

Reaching the car ahead of him, Anderson leant back against the passenger door and bit a chunk out of her bar. Cross ambled over, never in a rush unless it was on his way up the ranks. If he played his cards right—which he always seemed to do—he was likely to be the youngest Black DCI in the country. They worked well together when partnered up. Though it didn't happen as much as she'd like. If he was going places, she wanted to be right there in his slip stream. Whereas he only had one glass ceiling to crack, she had three to break through.

"Where's this truck?" Balling up the empty chocolate wrapper as he fobbed open the car.

"Bishop Hill, not far from the hospital."

A strange route for a tanker truck to take. She thought the bridge was unsuitable for HGVs but said nothing. If the driver was dead, there was really no point in throwing the highway code at him.

Four.

"I don't know what I saw, exactly." Callie sat on the back steps of an ambulance while a paramedic shone a light in her face. Someone had thrown a blanket across her shoulders to ward off the chills while a police officer took her statement.

Closing her eyes, she went back to the moment when she saw it. Although, what she saw—what she thought she saw—just didn't make any sense.

"Can you describe what you saw?" The uniform holding a notepad and pen.

Callie opened her eyes and looked up at the police officer. She was a petite twenty-something Asian woman—probably somewhere around her age.

That image in her head, if she said what she saw out loud, even she wouldn't believe it. "It was…it was really dark."

A flash of something briefly behind the constable's gaze like a light went out. "It was dark." Saying Callie's feeble words back to her before flipping closed her notepad.

"What about the cabin?" It had been bubbling up inside her the whole time. No one had asked her about what had happened, why she was there. Because of the dead driver, that's all they cared about. Well, if that's what it took, Callie would tell them something they wanted to hear. "He's about six foot tall, thin. Stringy. He's in his late forties, balding blond hair."

The constable was writing down her words. The description of the man who'd taken her. Not the thing she saw slither across the road and disappear into the woods. No one would believe that. Even Callie didn't want to. Nor the sudden lurch and thump as it flopped down from the tanker onto the cab roof. Through the windscreen, she saw a trail of murky liquid run down. She'd flinched back away as a flood of bile spilled across the glass, blurring the dark night outside. The cab shifted with a creak. That's when a white hulking thing slid down, bouncing slightly off the bonnet snapping one of the wipers off as it flopped toward the tarmac; a long, segmented tail whipping and flapping behind it.

"He didn't see me," her words coming out almost breathless, pointing toward the cab, "I was hiding in the back, behind the curtain." Because she knew what the next question would be. If the man she'd escaped from had come after her, then why wasn't she dead. Why wasn't she lying in the road with a hole through her stomach. The thought of it, of the worm creature, how she imagined it had burrowed its way through the truck driver. It made her gag.

She got up, the nurse who'd sat with her while they waited for the police to arrive, Grace, rushing to her, asking if she was okay. "I'd like to take her to the hospital, now." Grace talking to the officer with the notepad.

Callie couldn't see them, everything was suddenly blurry. It reminded her of looking through the cab windscreen at that thing as it slithered away, the trail of slime left in its wake smudging up the glass. A wave of heat enveloped her body followed by a shiver of cold. She was either going to faint or throw up.

"We just need to wait for the detectives, they're on their way."

What was taking them so long? Callie wanted to get out of there. Away from the tanker truck and its dead driver. Away from the dark country road and woods beyond. Away from the cabin and man who'd wanted to kill her. Away from whatever had spared her life.

Callie just wanted to go home.

Motioning to her, the constable pointed to one of the marked police cars blocking off the road. "You're welcome to sit and wait in my cruiser."

Meeting Grace's eye, they nodded in unison and wandered over to the car. It would be warmer and comfier than the metal steps of an open ambulance. Though the smell inside — when she pulled open the door—almost instantly made her reconsider. "What is that?" Looking to the nurse, like she might have an idea.

Grace smiled and shook her head. "You think that is bad, try an ambulance after a night shift." The knowing look which followed warmed Callie to her even more and convinced her to sit down. Both of them choosing to leave their doors ajar, obviously. Pulling the blanket tightly across her shoulders, she leaned back against the back seat and closed her eyes for a moment.

In a soft voice, Grace asked her, "What would you be doing now if you weren't here?"

The question opened her eyes. Between the front seats, a bright digital clock told her it was 02:38AM. She had no idea of the date. "Asleep probably." Turning to Grace. "What about you?"

A deep exhale of breath. "Watching

infomercials on TV."

That made Callie smile. "They're so cringy."

Grace's giggle was infectious. "Believe it or not, they help me sleep."

Callie never had trouble sleeping. When she was tired, she went to bed, laid her head and woke up the next morning. It was a mystery to her why people found switching off and resting troublesome. Though, after tonight, she was worried the pictures in her mind might keep her awake.

She shivered.

"Want me to close the door."

"God, no!" Making them both laugh.

Sounds of movement nearby outside flinched Callie's eyes open toward the ambulance. Two Black detectives were talking to the constable with the notepad. At least she guessed they were detectives; both of them wore dark suits instead of a uniform, crime scene tech coats or white forensic overalls, eyeing everything, nodding and asking questions.

"Finally."

Grace shifted next to her. "What is it?"

Nodding at them just as the constable did the same in their direction. All five locked eyes.

Unaware that she was doing it, Callie was gripping tightly onto the nurse's hand.

"I'm here."

At that moment, she was so glad somebody was. Though, when Grace heard what had happened to her tonight, heard what she'd seen, she was scared she'd want to get as far away from her as humanly possible.

Five.

"I'm Detective Cross, this is Detective Anderson." The man sat sideways in the driving seat in front of Grace.

Callie gripped her hand. She looked over at the girl urging her on with an encouraging smile, while squeezing back.

"Take your time, Miss Ireson. You're not in any trouble, okay? Just start from the beginning." Anderson, the female detective, sat shotgun, a friendly comforting smile across the seat backs.

The girl closed her eyes and began. "Someone grabbed me when I got out of work—picked me up and threw me in the back of their car." The words came out with a quiet urgency. A chilling encounter said simply with no hint of drama added.

"Where do you work?" Cross had a small note pad in his hand, writing.

Grace missed the name but recognized it as a restaurant in the city center. Her ex's new girlfriend had posted a selfie of them eating there on social media. Since then, it wasn't exactly top of her to eat list.

"What time was this?" Anderson asking the question, this time.

"Around six; I was covering the lunch shift." There were no follow up questions. The silence from the front urged the girl on. "He'd put a pillowcase over my head." Her voice hitching as she said the words. "It had a strong chemical smell, it…whatever it was…it knocked me out."

Grace swallowed hard, the grip on her left

hand so tight, it had gone numb. The poor girl.

"I woke up tied to a chair. It was cold. He'd stripped and gagged me."

Grace felt sick. Although she wanted to be here and be supportive, part of her wished she weren't. Wished that she'd driven a different way home tonight, the longer route. More than anything, she wanted to go to her daughter's room in her ex-husband's house, crawl into bed with her and all the stuffed bears and hold onto her tight.

"Did you get a look at him, at where he took you?"

Callie nodded, matter-of-factly. Grace noticed a single tear slide down her cheek as she repeated the description of the man she'd given to the officer outside the ambulance. In her head, Grace tried to match it to the people who came and went through her ward. Then through the men she worked with. There were so many men it could have been, it made her feel physically sick.

"What about the place?"

Taking a breath and wiping at her eyes, she told them about the wooden cabin in the woods she'd escaped from. Grace turned toward the wall of dark trees through the side window, the forest moving with a slight breeze. That man and the cabin were right out there. As the girl spoke, she could picture the debris littered floor of a rustic cabin, sparse furniture, and aged decor. A single chair in the center of a small room, one bare bulb hanging limp from the ceiling casting shadows over the girl bound to it and the man bent by the far wall, watching her. The chills she'd bundled up against moved around inside her clothing. It brought with it a moldy earthy smell which stung her nostrils.

The horror Callie must have felt wracked her chest and stomach muscles. The utter sheer dread and loneliness that she was probably going to die alone far from home and the ones who loved her, tore at Grace's insides. Without meaning to, she found herself weeping. Shoulders hitching, the sobs threatened to overtake her entire being.

Anderson saw what was going on with her and gave her a sad smile. How could she listen to people do this every day? Hearing the bad things that they'd been through and not break down each time? Grace wasn't a prude and had seen her share of horror stories in Accident and Emergency; had met children who were being abused and had to fight not to physically attack the monsters who sat next to them, holding their hands and lying to her. But hearing the reality of what one human had been through so matter-of-factly, filled her with a deep, hollow helplessness. That whatever she did would not stop this from happening again to someone else. That life and history unnecessarily repeated itself no matter what. That whatever she tried, there was nothing she could ever do to really protect or save her own little girl from men like this.

"How did you get away?" Cross' question broke her from reverie.

Grace needed to hear this. It was the good news part. The important bit.

"He untied me to take me to the bedroom."

Nausea rose up from her stomach at the thought of what that monster had planned.

"I was pulling away from him and, I guess, I kind of tripped and it brought him down."

Blind luck that a misstep toppled the beast. Grace saw the man's head crack on the hard wooden floor and the unreal shock on the girl's face. Of her wildly looking around for a way out, not stopping for breath but just running for her life.

Blinking out of her daze, Anderson tapping at the sat nav screen in the center console of the police car. "This is the closest building on the map." Looking back at Callie then tapping the screen until the rectangular building had enlarged to full. "You think this might be it?"

Callie nodded. "Yeah, I remember seeing the shed at the back and, when I got to the road, realized I'd followed the canal towpath."

A blue line marking the canal ran straight from the building to where they sat as the detective zoomed back out and set the destination.

"Can I take her to the hospital, now?" Grace getting in there before there was talk of taking Callie back to that place.

Next to her, the girl let go of her hand—the feeling roaring back in a buzz of pins and needles—to wipe her face and pull herself up out of the back seat.

The two detectives exchanged a look. "We haven't asked about the tanker truck."

Before anyone could say anything else, Callie blurted out that it was him. The man who had taken her, he was the one who'd killed the truck driver.

Another look crossed between the couple in the front seat. Anderson spoke this time. "The man from the cabin?"

Callie nodded, a little too vigorously.

"He did that?" Cross' question, eyebrows raised at the mess of a man left on the road.

That's when she broke down, hands covering her face, huge moaning breaths from the girl. Grace looked up at the two officers. Her eyes pleading with them to let her take this girl to the hospital. That she'd been through enough tonight.

"Miss Ireson, where did he go?" Anderson's careful voice.

"Back into the woods!" Callie almost screamed the words.

"Thank you, Callie." Cross' soft voice. It took all of Grace's strength not to break down right there and then in the back seat of the police car.

Six.

DS Anderson watched the girl and nurse make their way through the circus of technicians, emergency vehicles, and police tape. Those two women would be friends for life just because they happened to cross paths one night. It gave her a little spark of hope for humanity. A small reminder that there was still some good in the world.

"You buy any of that?" Cross standing next to her.

She shook her head. "Not about the tanker."

In front of them, a photographer was taking shots of the body. Bright flashes, stark against the night, brought out the vivid red spots within the pale dead flesh. Violent, fractured tears through the skin was not the work of another human being. At least, not one she'd ever encountered. Anderson blinked until the flare left the back of her eyes. It took as long as the high whine flash on the camera did to recharge.

"I think she came out of the woods, right over there," Cross pointing at a slight gap in the undergrowth and trees, near the hump of the canal bridge, "and stumbled into something going down." Moving around the photographer, Cross pointed again, this time at a circular metal object lying apparently discarded on the road. "What is that?"

Cross craned his head up at the tanker. He knelt, snagging a pair of blue nitrile gloves from a box by the broken body and roughly put them on. Without another word, he stood and took two strides toward the tanker then sprang up onto the metal ladder fixed to the side.

Anderson checked her surroundings for watchers. No one seemed to have noticed.

"Up here."

Shielding her face from the glare of another flash bulb, Anderson followed the sound of Cross' voice to the figure now standing on top of the trailer.

"It's some sort of cap or cover. The one up here's missing." As he made his way back down to the road.

"Think it was a robbery?"

Cross shook his head at her question. "Not unless there's money in raw sewage."

That explained the stench. "What about the driver? Could he have been carrying something he shouldn't have in the back of this thing?"

By the look on her partner's face, it was definitely a realistic consideration not to be immediately discounted. Anderson stepped up to the driver's door that had been left open. Nothing appeared to be missing. But then, she really had no idea what a typical truck driver generally carried around in their cab. Behind the curtain in the back was sparse. She went to duck back out when her eyes glanced off the dash cam fixed to the windscreen. "Dash cam," she called down to Cross.

Her partner pulled himself up with a smile on his face. "Nice spot."

Someone had turned the engine off, so the screen was black. An evidence tech must have taken the key as it was no longer in the ignition.

"You got your laptop in the boot?" Cross had been given a replacement laptop while IT were trying to fix his. With everything going on, he hadn't taken it out of the case yet, let alone his car.

While he disappeared to get it, Anderson un-cupped the device from the screen and turned it over to find the SD slot. Cross was soon back with his laptop open as it popped out.

"Here."

Once it booted up, Cross snapped in the card and swiveled the screen around so they could both see it. A folder popped up, a list of files syncing.

"Try the last one."

Cross dragged the cursor across the screen and double-clicked on the file name comprised of numbers and dashes. A video app appeared, a circle rotated in the center before it started to play.

Enlarged to fit the screen, the footage showed the same road but with no sound. A forest of trees on both sides, moving, main beams lighting up the tarmac like it was midday. After almost a minute, a pale shape ran out into its path.

"That's our girl."

Hands tied against her chest, holding closed a loose flapping shirt, while her bare legs ran across the road, the truck slowed, footage shuddering. They couldn't hear but saw exactly what's she was saying. *Help me*. After that, just empty road, lit up a hundred yards or so in front on screen.

"Can you adjust the sound?"

Cross pulled up the settings on the video. The sound had been turned off. It was all greyed out. At the bottom of the screen, a bar signifying how long was left showed about twenty minutes of footage remained.

"I'm skipping ahead."

Anderson watched the cursor slide across the bar. Though there was no change in the road on screen; she could see the surrounding tree line of the woods shimmy quicker as the playback was sped up.

"Stop."

Something flashed into view, knocking the dash cam askew and leaving them watching an obscure angle of the cab's interior. Cross dragged the bar back a touch, bringing the white flash back up again.

"There."

Hitting play, the detectives watched as a foam of watery goo spilled down the windscreen.

"What's that?"

Anderson didn't know.

A huge white blob then bounced into view, the dash cam taking a second to refocus on it. It made them both jump back. The way it sprung onto the hood, it must have dropped down from the cab roof. The impact knocked the dash cam askew.

"Go back."

Cross slid the bar back and clicked play. "What is that?"

It looked to Anderson like a huge white snake, but fatter. Cross wound back the footage, again. On a second watch, the body was segmented like a worm. It moved like an accordion being played.

Cross shared her view. "It looks like a damn worm."

The video played again. Both of them hunched, heads down close to the laptop screen.

"It came from the tanker."

It was the only logical explanation. But Anderson had a more pressing question. "Where'd it go?"

Leaping down from the cab, she had her

mobile out, swiping the screen up for the torch function. It flashed on, illuminating the road. Right in front of the grill, the light picked up a wet smudge on the tarmac.

"What you got?" Cross stood next to her, head down close to where the light splayed.

Where the beam caught it, areas seemed to glisten and sparkle. "I think it's a slime trail."

"But worms don't leave a trail."

"This one does."

Although only brief, she was certain what she saw on the footage was not a slug.

"Where'd it go?"

Lifting the phone, Anderson shone it a little higher along the road. The trail led away, straight ahead from the cab toward the canal bridge across the road. "This way."

One standing each side of the trail, Cross and Anderson followed the slime until it stopped at the bridge.

"So, what now?"

Cross wiped a hand over his face and shook his head. "I'll call pest control."

That made her laugh—snort through her nose. "You do that, and I'll check out the cabin."

Seven.

"In two-hundred yards, turn left."

Anderson didn't see the turn ahead, but flicked the indicator down and slowed the car, anyway. A gap in the tree line appeared in the headlights and she took it. From the tarmac country road, the car bumped down a single lane, gravel track lined with trees and bushes. A checkered flag appeared on screen. Up ahead, the headlights wavered, picking out nothing in particular. Low hanging tree branches and thorns scratched against both sides of the car, making her check the rearview.

Holding the wheel firmly in both hands, Anderson navigated around a slight bend where the rear of another vehicle caught in the main beam. It was a long black estate car with a princess on board sticker in the rear window. Looking ahead of it stood the cabin. Dark apart from a faint glimmer of light leaking through the main window.

Anderson parked behind the car, making

sure to block it in so whoever was inside couldn't get away, should the sudden urge strike them. Parked across the lane, the handbrake went on and Anderson got out, taking the keys with her. Phone in one hand, she went back to the torch function and shone it ahead of her. With no streetlights or moon visible, the darkness out there was almost absolute.

There were no sounds but the rustle of the surrounding forest and her work boots scrunching against the gravel. She reached the front door and knocked, hearing nothing else but the echoing stillness which followed. At the main window, she cupped her hands around her face as she peered inside. One lone bulb dangled from the ceiling, pooling light into the center of the room. A single straight-backed wooden chair lay on its side. Nothing else but shadows lurked around the periphery. To one direction was an archway into what she guessed was the kitchen area from the blocks of dark shadow fixed around waist height inside.

Following the boundary, past the car, Anderson headed for the rear of the property, torch light swiping the ground in front of her. Tall grass crumpled a path from the makeshift driveway where a small shed came into view. It was the one she showed Callie on the sat nav. The one she told her she'd remembered seeing when she got free.

The door swung open in a slight breeze, shaking the surrounding trees and shrubbery, causing her to slow her advance.

It was just the wind.

A thin path led from the shed to the cabin, her phone brought out a glittering crimson sparkle amongst the grass. The sight of blood quickened her pulse, catching her breath. Checking her surroundings, she used her foot to nudge open the shed door and peered inside.

It was an outhouse. The lone porcelain toilet inside, marked with dark stains which splattered across the floor. Using her torch, Anderson followed the trail back to the cabin's rear door. Which, also, had been left ajar.

Stepping over the shiny trail of blood mixed with slime, she walked toward the cabin, eyes everywhere all at once. She wasn't about to be victim number three. Anderson moved just inside the back door. A body lay on the kitchen floor, blocking her entry.

"Hello?" Instantly regretting speaking as soon as she heard her own high voice in the surrounding stillness.

Shouldering the door, she pushed against it steadily, easing it further open as it shifted the legs on the floor aside. It was male, tall from the long sprawling body. Callie had described her abductor as stringy and that's exactly the word which came to mind when Anderson looked down at him. At least he wouldn't be hurting anyone else.

The glittery blood trail stopped at the man's back which faced her, moving the door inwards had rolled him further onto his left side. She pushed again, the door catching on the backs of his thighs.

"Hey?" Anderson's voice was quieter, this time, as she scanned the dark kitchen, looking for the slime trail. Her torch light picking up nothing else and no other movement. Pushing through the gap she'd made, Anderson stepped over the man and squeezed inside. Bending down, she felt for a pulse. Instead, what she felt moving around underneath the slick skin, pulled her hand away, fast. Pointing her phone at his neck, she saw the squirming, wriggling, swarming forms zig zagging beneath and up into the man's hairline.

Frozen in place, her eyes peaked at the cheekbones which became deformed as the finger-length worms pushed their way up toward the brain. For a second, Anderson thought she saw the man's head move, but knew it was just from the barrage of bodies flooding upwards that had rocked the head back on its dead neck.

But then he did move. The wobbly torch light specking off the man's blank eyes as they blinked open and spun to stare at her. Before she could react, a cold hand reached up and gripped hard around her wrist. The one holding onto the phone, which now wrenched backward, sending the face, those pale eyes, and grimace grin into darkness.

Anderson jumped back, tugging free her arm and catching the heel of her boot against the bottom of a corner cabinet next to the door. It tripped her outside onto the long grass. Scrambling up, she brushed herself down, backing away from the cabin, the writhing body, and the slick feel of the man's swarming neck still on her fingers.

The phone in her hand pulsed to life with the ringtone too loud in the quiet night air. She flung it down an instant before stooping back to pick it up.

It was Cross.

The dead man in the cabin was floundering on the kitchen floor, trying to get his legs under him. She answered the call, still backing away from the cabin.

"Talk to me." His voice all static against the loud pounding in her ears.

"It's here." Watching as the dead man struggled to his knees beyond the open back door. She looked down at her fumbling fingers, hitting the icon for loudspeaker so she could point the light on him but still hear her partner. Even from a short distance away, his pale skin appeared fluid with movement.

"The worm-thing?" Concern in his voice. It sounded alien to her. Cross was usually so calm and collected.

Anderson spun on her heels, hearing the wind build up and blow through the trees behind her. *Where was it?*

"Anderson, talk to me; what's going on?" He was moving, rushing somewhere; she could hear the breaths coming out like he was running.

"It's been here…it's attacked…they're inside him…"

"Get to your car, lock yourself inside, I'm en route, okay?" More rustling sounds over the phone in her ear.

In the torch light, the dead man had his hands on the kitchen countertop. He was pulling himself up on unsteady knees. Anderson turned and fled, her boots scuffling against the dry ground, running on legs that didn't feel like her own. She didn't stop until her car was in sight and she was braced against the driver's door, scrambling for her keys with the phone still in her hand but almost dropping it and everything in the process.

Falling into the car, Anderson pulled the door shut and locked it, feeling the shivers leave her body in droves. Punching the key into the ignition after missing the first couple of times she tried, she twisted it while stamping on the clutch and forcing the gear into reverse. Screaming backwards, completely forgetting to remove the handbrake, the full force of her right foot on the accelerator pedal. Her eyes never leaving the cabin, waiting for the dead man to appear around the side of the building and come for her as it got smaller.

Eight.

The drive over to the hospital was a quiet one. After baring everything in front of Grace, Callie was in no mood to share. She supposed the nurse felt just as uncomfortable, hearing and knowing things about a total stranger they normally wouldn't share. How did someone make small talk after that?

Callie didn't mind the silence. The radio was on low—tuned to some eighties station—it took her mind off what was going on in her life. Soon the wall of trees gave way to hedgerows, a few spread out houses with streetlights. Seeing the orange glow approach settled her. It had felt like forever since she'd seen civilization. It calmed her, helped her feel everything would soon be alright.

"Almost there." The quiet had gotten too much for the nurse.

Callie smiled across at her. The space between them—past the center console—felt like an abyss where less than an hour before, they'd been holding on to each other's hands like they were the only people who mattered. The difference made her look away and back out the passenger window.

The truth was, Callie didn't feel the need to go to the hospital. Apart from a few scrapes and bruises, physically she was fine. It was just that the offer to go felt like a good out from the back of that police car and, if she was being honest with herself, she didn't want to be alone. A cast of people in a brightly lit waiting room felt close to heaven right then. To be back home, alone, in her flat knowing that man was still out there, waiting for him to come after her, filled her with absolute dread.

With a bump, Grace steered them up onto a sloping access road to the hospital. The bright lights made her squint. She'd be safe here.

"When we get in, I'll find you some spare scrubs to wear."

Callie smiled at Grace. "Thank you." She'd never worn them before and guessed they felt rough against her skin. Looking down at the baggy T-shirt barely reaching her mid-thigh, she'd willingly wear anything to cover herself.

Pulling at the hem, she thought about the truck driver and how she'd gotten him killed. If she hadn't flagged him down, he might still be alive. Closing her eyes, for the life of her, she couldn't recall if he wore a wedding ring. What if he had a wife waiting up at home? Or kids asleep in their beds who would miss their dad in the morning and every other?

In comparison, there was no one waiting at home for her to return. Surviving in place of him stung her chest and made her ears burn.

"All set?" Grace turned to her, pulling the key from the ignition and reaching back to open her door.

Callie looked up through the windscreen. They were parked up behind the main hospital building. It was a four-story, grey concrete structure with the occasional bright window amongst most that were blacked out. "Yeah."

She got out, looking back at where they'd

reverse parked. Behind a low wall, the murkiness chilled her. Beyond bushes lay the dark waters of the canal. It must have been the same stretch of water which ran past the cabin right to the road they'd just come from.

A splash reeled her back against the car.

"You okay?" Grace's hand on her shoulder, steadied her.

Callie smiled. She still hadn't told anyone what she saw. What she was afraid of. Whatever that thing was had escaped over the canal bridge, given the miles of waterways which networked across Britain, what were the chances of the worm thing being where they were now?

Nine.

Grace Wan led Callie through the back entrance, along a long corridor and into the nurses' changing room. The girl was around a foot taller than her, so guessed her spare set of scrubs would fit her. "Here you go." Pulling them out and shaking them open.

Callie held onto them, not moving.

"You okay?" A stupid question, really, as it left her mouth. Of course she wasn't okay. If a madman had abducted her, knocked her out and tied her up in a deserted cabin deep in the woods, she guessed she'd feel a little out of sorts herself.

Grace turned around as Callie stripped off the T-shirt. "You want something to eat?"

"I'm fine." Came the quiet, hollow reply.

"A drink? There's a vending machine out in the corridor."

Against the rustle of clothing. "Yeah, a coffee would be nice, thanks."

She'd have one herself. Turning to face the girl, stood there in her green scrubs which were a little short on the ankles and wrists, but otherwise covered her. She told her, "Be right back."

Out in the hall, she went right, making a beeline for the drinks machine.

"Can't get enough of the place, huh?" Gwen, another nurse on the opposite shift, clocked her as she walked through carrying a yellow box of sharps.

"There's been an accident up the road."

Her friend's eyes widened. "The tanker

truck? You were there?"

News travelled fast. When the ambulance had showed up, Grace had nodded a greeting to one of the new paramedics—Bob she thought his name was—and helped Sharon see to Callie. They must have come back while she was sat in the back of the police car.

Gwen stepped closer. "They said the driver was torn to pieces."

A flash of memory stiffened Grace. Hollowed out was more like it. The hole in his stomach looked as though something had burrowed through it. Callie had said a man had done that. The one who had abducted her. Bracing a hand against the coffee machine, she took a breath.

"You okay, Grace?"

Her vision had wavered. The corridor had gone a little blurred and made Gwen a spec on the horizon, lost in the distance.

A hand on her shoulder and Gwen returned right next to her. "Why don't you go home; I'll take care of the girl you brought in. When did you last eat something?"

It was impossible to lie to a work colleague when they were nurses, too. Grace nodded at the vending machine. "I'm fine, honestly. I'll get something out of here."

"Make sure you do." Gwen's parting words as she left for the incinerator.

Putting in all her change, Grace hit the buttons for a white coffee. While it was pouring, she looked over the vending machine options. It had to be chocolate. She'd pick out a bar with whatever change was left from getting the drinks. The return coins rattled down into the tray. Grace plucked them out and put them into the vending machine. As she hit the selection, the lights on the machine and above her, warbled.

Not another power cut?

Above her, the ceiling lights throbbed then went out. The hallway descending into darkness for a few seconds before the backup generators lit. A low groan went up from the nearby ward. Behind her, the changing room door swung inwards. Grace turned to see Callie's wide eyes and handed her the plastic cup of coffee. "Just a power cut. We get them all the time."

That and the hot cup seemed to calm her. She turned back to the vending machine. It had swallowed her money.

Damn it.

Grace slammed against the machine. It beeped and the hallway went black. For a second, she thought she'd done that. But, no, the back up generators were down, too.

Why tonight?

Turning back to the open door and girl's open mouth, Grace told Callie to stay put while she went down to the generator shed to see if she could help out.

Ten.

"I'm telling you, he was right here." Anderson pointed inside the back doorway of the cabin.

Cross aimed the light at the ground, sweeping it across the kitchen floor. Just like the trail they'd followed from the tanker truck to the canal bridge, whatever it was seemed to glisten.

Anderson had her own phone trained amongst the long grass. Where had he gone? From the outhouse, she moved the light into the surrounding trees, then off toward where the canal must be. Nothing, no movement and no blood. "Maybe he's still inside?" She turned around. But Cross was no longer there. Through the back window, there was a glimmer of torch light visible. Feeling suddenly vulnerable, on show out there on her own, Anderson followed her partner inside, making sure to step over the red slime patch by the open door.

"In here."

She followed his voice into another room. Cross was standing in the middle of the main living area next to the overturned chair. That's where the girl had been bound. Two snapped zip ties lay discarded on the floor. They were the same color as the ones found in the cab. But his phone wasn't pointing down at the chair nor the ties. The torch light was directed to an open doorway at the far side of the cabin. And at the drops of red slime that disappeared through it into the dark.

"He went that way."

Ducking back into the kitchen, Anderson looked around for a weapon. A few dirty plates and dishes on the countertop and in the sink. Pulling open drawers, she rifled inside for a knife; anything long or sharp. But there was nothing.

"Here."

She turned around to see Cross holding out a wooden rolling pin. In his other hand, he had a broom.

"You ready?"

Anderson nodded. Although she was anything but. She didn't want to be back inside this cabin. Not with a man who abducted women. Especially those types of men who were dead and had worms crawling through their faces. "After you."

With a smirk, Cross went for the door, leading them where the abductor had tried to take the girl only hours before. Only, she had never made it that far. Callie Ireson had gotten lucky and got free. And if anyone needed it, it was her.

They crossed the room slowly; Anderson eyed the kitchen then front door. Through the main window, overlooking the front of the property, she could see their cars blocking in the abductor's only means of escape. They had him cornered. Whether it was really wise to corner an animal was a question that she guessed would be answered soon enough.

Cross was through the door. A short hallway lay beyond with two options, one on either side. The nearest door to their right was part way open. She caught Cross' eye. He switched his grip so the broom he was carrying was in his most dominant hand. Anderson already had her weapon in her right. She raised it up so the drop would be easier. Then nodded at Cross that she was ready.

Using the tip of the broom handle, Cross nudged the nearest door fully open, flashing the phone inside. Anderson shifted closer, holding up her own phone to light up the areas of the room Cross' torch didn't touch.

They were in a box room. A stark, empty box room. All that was in there was a hulking antique-looking wardrobe against the far wall. There was really no room for anything else. And, unlike the other rooms they'd searched so far, there was no debris on the floor. Just a threadbare rug.

"What d'you think's in there?"

Anderson was wondering the exact same thing. Only she was the one creeping toward it. There were no spots of blood in the room with them. A dead man wouldn't be hiding inside an old wardrobe, would he?

"If there's no back to this, don't be surprised."

It was funny; she could not imagine Cross having ever read a children's book.

Looking up, he had leant the broom against the side of the wardrobe, keeping it still within easy reach. His free hand flexed as it went to open the door.

"Wait." Anderson hissed as she rushed forward. She had the worst feeling that whatever was in there wasn't good. That once they opened it, there was no going back.

The light from her phone lit up her partner's hand as it closed around the metal handle. One quick turn was all it would take to twist it open. The noise of the rusty mechanism creaking around was too loud in the quiet gloom. It made her check the hallway. Although she knew no one was there.

"It's locked."

Turning back to Cross as he twisted and pulled at the rattling handle. Below it was a keyhole. The sound of breaking glass split the air. It came from down the hall. From the last door at the end of the cabin. The one that was closed. Just like the wardrobe.

They were out, across the hall and rushing through the closed door in an instant. Cross with his broom raised and Anderson clutching her rolling pin. Two detectives inside an isolated cabin, chasing after a dead man.

Curtains flapped across the shattered window, the red slime trail disappearing through it. A single rusty metal camp bed took up the space in the cramped room. Compared to the other box room, this was in disarray. It also had a smell that Anderson recognized, it brought to mind a fatal car wreck she'd attended years ago when still in uniform. A moment she'd always associated with death.

Cross had his phone hovering over the bed, the main focal point in the room. The bare mattress was stained maroon in places. Strewn around it were what looked like discarded old rags. Shining a light on them, she could see they weren't rags but pieces of ripped clothing.

"Our girl wasn't the first."

Outside, a car engine screamed to life.

They locked eyes. Both knew it was their

man getting away. A crash followed by another roar of the engine. He was ramming his way out. Barreling across the room and out along the corridor, they headed toward the noise. In the glare of headlights, they stood in the living room as the car bumped forward, shaking the cabin structure before it reversed back, slamming their cars aside.

Anderson went for the back door while Cross took the front. Racing to stop the man's escape, a corner of the kitchen counter caught her toe and the trip flung her forward, sprawling down onto the patch of red slime in the doorway, Anderson's head cracked against the door in a flare and buzz of firelight.

Before she lost consciousness, she heard Cross call out and an engine screech then another smash of breaking glass.

Eleven.

Callie sat drinking coffee in the dark of the nurses' changing room. Warmth from the plastic cup radiated up her hands then out through into her extremities. Although it did nothing for the cool wooden bench beneath her, or the feeling that chilled her. That tonight was far from over.

She said she would stay put for Grace. The nurse had stopped and pulled her out of her own isolated horror. The woman had stayed with her through the police interview and brought her here without being asked. She'd even given a stranger her clothes to wear and brought her a drink. It was the least Callie could do.

But once the nurse came back, Callie would get out of her life. Get a good night's sleep in her own bed rather than pull her out of her everyday and away from everything of hers. If it wasn't for her, Grace would be at home watching infomercials. Going through her usual bedtime routine instead of being back at work in the dead of night, wandering the darkened corridors helping to fix the lights.

Movement from across the room zapped her back inside the cabin. Tied to that chair unable to move. Tasting the thick sweaty fabric stuffed inside her mouth. Suppressing the gag reflex as she peered out through a tear in the pillowcase over her head. At a shadow slipping apart from the surrounding darkness and out, standing in front of her. A tall, stringy shape towering over her, looking down holding onto a wooden rolling pin.

A rolling pin?

"Morning sunshine." A gravelly voice stripped of all emotion. The vibrations sent tendrils up her bare upper arms.

In a flash, his free hand whipped off the material covering her head. The sudden brightness had Callie squinting. She was glad because she didn't want to see his face. In the movies, they always killed the ones who could identify them.

"Look at me." That same, flat gravelly voice. It drilled right through into her very soul.

Against her chest, she felt it. Blinking open her eyes, she looked down at the rolling pin prodding her. Slowly, he brought it up, tilting back her chin until her eyes had nowhere else to go but on him.

"You're such a pretty thing."

It was a shame the same could not be said about him. A thin, drawn, pale face. Hollowed out eyes staring down at her from under the low ridge of his sweeping forehead. Thinning light hair receded all the way up. And that was nowhere near as bad as the grin he wore. All teeth and curled, thin lips.

Now that she was looking at him, Callie decided to stare. She was going to memorize every single feature on his middle-aged, ugly face. Because she was getting out of there. This wasn't how it was going to end for her. This man, whatever he had planned for her, it was not going to go his way. Callie would get free and survive, somehow. So she wanted to be sure she never forgot him. Not one detail of what he looked like so she could give the police a description of a monster.

Ceiling lights flickering brought her out of her head. The power was back on and she was no longer alone. Looking down at the half-drunk cold coffee clutched in her hands. The muddy sludge looked exactly like the taste in her dry mouth. She sat up and went over to a sink and tipped what was left down the drain and ran the tap. Swilling out the small plastic cup before filling it with water and draining the lot in a few long gulps.

A crunch and thud from the line of cubicle

stalls brought her attention away from the sink and swirling water. Was someone else in there with her? If so, they'd been unusually quiet throughout the lights going out and loss of power.

"Hello?" Callie asked, feeling like an expendable extra in a bad horror movie.

No reply other than a hollow tinny ceramic chime and splash of water from across the wet room. She went over to the nearest of three stalls and nudged open the door. It swung inward with a creak. No one was inside. Taking a step forward, she craned her neck to peer down into the toilet bowl. The water pooled at the bottom whirled a little like it had just been flushed. A curling sucking sound accompanied the sight of water being drained down to leave a discolored empty bowl.

The floor beneath her heaved and shifted while a line of splintering cracks appeared in the smooth white tiles, widening out from the first stall towards her. Callie jumped back, out of the cubicle, and over the tear which had opened up underneath her. Torrents of steam hissed from the jagged chasm. Her eyes went from that to the sound of high-pressure water escaping from the pipework feeding the toilet cisterns fixed along the walls. The whole room shook, tipping her off balance and onto the ground. On hands and knees, Callie scrambled away from the chaos until her back was pressed up against the wall between the row of sinks. From there, she looked on as the cisterns shot out, crashing through the stall walls.

A warble rattled the building like a mini earth tremor. From her vantage, sitting on the cold tiles, gave her the perfect view of the creature emerge from the depths, boiling up with the murky sewage overflow. A gust of rot, shit, and piss hit her, along with it. Just like she remembered when sat stationary inside the cab, it was about the size and length of her thigh and had a pale white—almost smooth looking—skin. The tip of its head was domed. Callie daren't move now it had her in its sights. Not when she saw those red piercing eyes surface. They looked at her, staring straight into her eyes, pinning her to the spot. Slowly, evenly, it rose up until its mouth came into focus. When she saw the jagged, hooked teeth gape—long tendrils of thick saliva separating them—it took her breath away.

Then the lights went out. And Callie
screamed.

Twelve.

Leaving Callie where she was, Grace headed
along the dark corridor. It was quiet at this late
hour. Quieter than normal considering the recent
cutbacks. Most of the rooms were left empty and
disused. While whole sections of the hospital
had been abandoned and left unstaffed. Key
patient services such as maternity and pediatrics
had been transferred to other, more modern
facilities within the same Trust. It was sad.

Grace had worked there for almost fifteen
years. And it was like the place was slowly
dying. There was talk of closure. Of moving
everything away and leaving the site derelict. If
they shifted all the staff to another hospital, the
nearest one would take her twenty miles out of
her way. The added cost of getting to work
would hardly make it worth her while getting out

of bed in the morning. And, as for her daughter, forget being able to get home in time to pick her up from school. Her ex would be in his element with that one and back in his solicitor's office drafting another application for sole custody.

But she couldn't worry about what might never happen now. Not with more pressing things which were actually happening all around her. Women being abducted, almost killed, were far more important, as was the power being out at a hospital full of patients and staff.

Walking past the incinerator, Grace paused to peer inside the open door for Gwen.

Where was she?

At the end of the corridor, she could see that the fire door was ajar, as was the maintenance room opposite. Quickening her steps, she ducked inside maintenance to see if either John or Keith were there. But it was empty. The generator shed was outside, between the main building and canal towpath. Whichever one of them were on shift tonight were most likely out there trying to get the power back online.

Pushing through the fire exit, she spotted Gwen crouched down over a shape not far from the dividing wall. Grace broke into a trot, calling out to her friend.

It was Keith, lying on his back, groaning.

"He's been bit," Gwen told her. "He said something came out of the water and attacked him."

With wide eyes, Grace looked down at the gaping wound on his right calf. Squatting to get a better angle, she could make out what looked like an oval gash that could be a bite.

Laying a hand on his chest, she asked Keith, "Did you get a good look at it?"

His head was pulled back in agony, eyes squeezed shut tight and mouth stretched wide in a soundless scream.

"I don't think he's with it."

He did seem out of it. "We need to get him inside."

Gwen nodded and looked for the old wheelchair the maintenance crew used to move their tools around and sit in when they had a cigarette break by the canal. It was overturned next to the knee-high dividing wall.

While she went to get it, Grace pulled Keith up into a sitting position. As she moved him, the change in pressure caused the wound to gush blood. The man howled, arching his back. As she cradled his head, Grace felt the eeriest of sensations. Like Keith's skin was crawling.

Gwen was next to her with the wheelchair and stooped to lift him from the opposite side. It pushed the odd feeling from her head.

"Ready, after three?"

Grace nodded, braced Keith's arm around her shoulders, and lifted with Gwen as she counted to three. Struggling together with the weight and the man tipping back his body, they got him into the chair with some effort.

Pushing a groaning man over uneven ground wasn't easy. Grace had to stop and hold Keith in the chair as the pain made him flop around. He managed to get hold of her and hissed out a sound that sounded like 'snake.'

"A snake bit you?"

The pain seemed to rock him back in the chair and knock him out.

Exchanging puzzled looks, they got him back to the fire door and wheeled him inside.

"What are we going to do with the lights?"

Grace looked back at the maintenance room. She had helped John when the breakers had tripped a couple of times due to the old MRI machine upstairs. "You take him into A and E, and I'll see if anything's been tripped."

Gwen went ahead, meandering along the corridor as she pushed the unconscious maintenance man. She watched them go until the darkness swallowed them whole. In the maintenance room, Grace pulled out her mobile and swiped to the torch function. It lit up a hole in the darkness and tunneled it toward a big red fuse box fixed to the wall. Something had tripped them out. She smiled and flicked them all back up to the on position.

And, just like that, the power surged.

On one of the work benches was a red metal diesel can, written across it was the word *'Generator.'* That explained why the generator hadn't fired up when the power tripped out. She would refill the tank for Keith, go and check on Callie then go home and get some sleep. She had to be back here this afternoon.

Snagging the can, Grace headed for the generator shed. Everyone called it that even though the engine was housed in a squat concrete bunker. She pushed through and flicked on the light at shoulder height. Then stopped.

There was a trail of what looked like blood from the doorway all the way over to the generator itself. There was a darker patch by the tank. As she crossed the room, something in the stains seemed to glimmer like glitter. Keith must have taken the top off to refill it but couldn't find the diesel can.

Was this where the snake bit him?

Grace looked around the room, checking the corners, but saw nothing. Bringing up the can, she unscrewed the cap and went to tip it into the tank when what she saw stopped her.

Behind the tank, all bunched up, was a mass of pale, white, jelly-like pods. Each one was about the size of a small lime but with hundreds collected together they filled the space against the back wall. Some of them had split open and were oozing the same speckled fluid that had been trailed along the concrete floor. It smelled bad—sharp like ammonia but also sour like expired seafood—she covered her nose with her free hand.

What were these?

Eggs?

As a kid, her big brother's best mate had a pet snake. But what she was seeing looked nothing like she remembered. These were fleshy, pulsating sacks that were translucent in places. Looking closer, she could see shapes squirming around inside. They were long and jerked like baby snakes. Although no kind of snake Grace had ever seen.

Movement rocked her head down. From the corner of her eye, she saw something shift. She flinched. Diesel spilled down upon the bulging egg sacks. When the flammable liquid sloshed over, they hissed, and steam rose up stinging her eyes.

Grace backed up, righting the canister as the squealing started.

More pods cracked and split open. Whatever was inside, sprang free. On impulse, she upturned the whole can, dousing everything in fuel. Plumes of acrid colored smoke billowed up, intensifying the eerie squeals from within. It pushed her back further until there was enough distance. Then she flung the entire metal can and fled the shed as the power went out.

Thirteen.

A rocking movement woke her. Anderson tried to sit up but was restrained.

Cross appeared over her, smiling. "Well, good morning, sunshine."

She was in the back of an ambulance. A moving ambulance. "What's going on?"

"You blacked out."

Everything came back to her in a flash. The cabin. Their dead man. She remembered tripping, going for the back door. "Did you get him?" Anderson blinked and saw that he was all banged up.

"Nah, he got me." Easing himself back down with a wince. She waited while her partner swallowed. "Got me with his car." Cross gave her an apologetic smile. "I got uniforms on it when I found you spark out on the kitchen floor."

Anderson dropped her head back and

closed her eyes. It was her fault, all of this. If she hadn't scarpered. If she hadn't been spooked, Callie's attacker wouldn't have gotten free. And she wouldn't be strapped to a bed in the back of an ambulance.

Slowly, she raised herself up onto her elbows and reached down to unclip the binds. A paramedic went to stop her.

"I'm fine."

"You might have a concussion," she was told. "Just lie back until we get to where we're going, please."

Anderson relented. She had a job to do but then, so did they. "Okay." Holding up her hands and lying back down.

Cross' mobile went off. "Yeah?" A pause. "What you got?"

Anderson looked over at him as he spoke.

His eyebrows went up, then he nodded. "That was his last stop?" Looking over at her. "Okay, get someone over there, I want to know what the hell he picked up." Pocketing his phone, Cross dusted his hands. He did that when he was thinking of what to say. It seemed to help him collect his thoughts. "We've traced the tanker driver back to his last pick up."

Anderson was paying attention.

"A waste treatment waystation beneath an abandoned research facility," Cross said.

The worm. "You think there might be more of those…things?" There was every chance.

Cross shrugged. "At least we know where it came from."

Now, they just needed to find it and work out how to kill it. If that was even possible.

From the side window, she could make out the looming shadows of the hospital.

The ambulance slowed. "Not again." Anderson followed the voice to the driver up front.

"What is it?" Cross got up to peer through the window into the cab.

The driver turned to them. "Another power cut."

"Perfect." One of the paramedics, this time.

They were there. After a few bumps, they were on site and Anderson waited for them to stop so she could get out and get this over with so they could get on and wrap things up.

"Anything on our man?"

Cross, head down on his phone, looked up

and shook his head. "There's roadblocks in place, he won't get far."

The back doors were flung open. Anderson lay still while they got her out and wheeled the bed along the carpark under the awning and into the back entrance to the Accident and Emergency department. As they passed through into the building, the subdued gloom gave way to bright strip lights overhead as the power roared back on. A cheer went up and Anderson spotted people sat around waiting for their call and a couple of hospital staff standing behind a desk. She was taken around the back of the main waiting room, through a narrow corridor past an occasional bench and up to a vacant cubicle with a long blue curtain representing the fourth wall. The two paramedics went about unstrapping her and getting what was needed to check her vitals and, hopefully, discharge her from their care.

When she turned around, Cross wasn't with her. The female paramedic held up a pen light. "Can you follow the light, please?"

She did as she was told. Looking left, right, up, down.

"Any headaches, blurred vision, dizziness?"

She shook her head. Everything was fine. Her knee was a bit sore and her left wrist, where she'd braced herself when she fell. Otherwise, Anderson was fine. Hungry, tired, but fine.

"I want you to go straight home, okay, Detective?"

Anderson nodded on impulse, though she had no intention of pausing her search. There was a dead man on the loose and a killer worm attacking people. "Thanks." As she got up to leave. The curtain was pulled aside and there stood Cross.

"Ready to go?"

She was and followed him from the line of cubicles and out into the corridor. "How we getting back?" As Cross had accompanied her in the ambulance, they were without transport.

"One of the uniforms are on their way."

They reached the side door which automatically slid apart. Anderson stepped through but Cross remained still. "I don't believe it."

She followed his outstretched arm to the jet-black estate car parked crookedly across three bays. There was a new dent in the bonnet and driver's side wing but the 'Princess on board' sticker was still in the back window. "He's here."

A commotion behind them broke the spell. That and the lights going out spun them both around.

"What's happened to Keith?" A concerned call from the paramedic who treated Anderson.

"Something came out of the canal and bit him."

The detectives locked eyes.

Fourteen.

Almost wrenching the doors from their hinges, Callie made it out into the corridor and ran. Not the same way the nurse had taken, but back toward the main entrance. Somehow, whatever had escaped from the tanker had followed her here. She'd already escaped a madman intent on killing her tonight. She wasn't about to let some creature end her, either.

Rushing past the shadows of closed doors

and darkened windows, up ahead was the main entrance and A and E department waiting room. Although still steeped in darkness, the glazed frontage of the building at least allowed in some moonlight which raised the gloom. Callie ran for it and the safety of other people as the tremors continued to rumble through the ground beneath her.

That thing, when it burrowed up from the sewers, it seemed bigger to her. Paler, wider, meaner. She blinked the memory aside and darted for the open double doors which gave way to freedom. In her head, she debated stopping to warn whoever was in charge or just to keep on going until she was safely far enough away from all of this. She knew the right answer and angled her footfalls toward the main reception desk that now came into view. That was, until a long, tall shadow fell across the doorway.

It was those blank sunken dark eyes and thin lips within that pale face that stopped her cold. When she saw the man who had taken her step out into her path, the memory of bounding through the undergrowth and trees came back to her with a jolt. Suddenly, she was right back there in the faded light of the forest still running for her life.

How had he found her?

Of all the places she could be, had he miraculously found his way back to where she was or did he simply expect her to arrive at the hospital and had lain in wait?

Skidding to a halt, reaching out and grasping for the walls to stop her, Callie backtracked against the buffered floor and changed course. She could've kept going and barreled through him, but the shock of seeing him there had sucked all the momentum from her. If she'd gone on, he would have got to her before even making it to the open doorway. The only way forward for her was to go back. Not all the way back to the changing room, just enough to get some distance from him so she could find an open door and barricade herself on the other side of it.

As she spun on the spot, almost slipping to the ground as her feet found traction, she saw another shadow approach.

"Callie!" It was Grace rushing headlong toward her. "I told you to stay put!"

With that, the changing room door behind her exploded out from the wall in a cloud of splintered wood, plaster, and debris. Both women ducked as the force of the blast rocked the air nearby.

Just past the vending machine was a set of double doors. "This way!" Grace screamed as the nurse reached for Callie's hand and shouldered the doors inward.

Once through, they flung themselves against the doors, Grace dropping to the ground to snap the floor bolts into place while Callie turned and jumped up to secure the ceiling locks. They came together to ram closed the main bar lock then pushed off to lose themselves within the myriad of rooms beyond.

Callie wanted to tell her about what she'd seen rising up from beneath the earth. About the creature that had escaped from the tanker and killed its driver. But to do that meant admitting that she'd lied to the police and to her.

They passed through a ward with its own mini waiting area and down along a shorter corridor which led to a series of consulting rooms. All of them had doors, places to hide or objects they could use as weapons. Grace led her to the furthest one. It was darker inside with the blinds drawn.

Callie twisted the lock and went over to the bed set against the opposite wall. It had wheels. Kicking off the brakes, she pulled it from the corner and pushed it over to block the door, snapping the wheel brakes back on.

Dull light seeped into the room as the blinds were drawn up by the nurse. The room held a long metal desk, a couple of chairs, two filing cabinets, and a small sink. Callie threw herself at the desk, wrenching open drawers, spilling the pots, and flipping trays to arm herself. Grace just stood back against the window staring straight ahead, not looking at anything in particular.

"Hey?" Edging closer to the nurse. "There's something I need to tell you."

Her voice had flicked a switch. Grace blinked and smiled across at Callie. It was a warm smile. One that understood what she was about to say and why she had to say it. With a shake of her head, Grace told her it didn't matter.

Standing there, holding onto a metal letter opener like it was a blade, Callie felt the urge to hug this woman.

Lights flashed across the walls; a red and blue pulse that rolled from ceiling to floor, from left to right. At the window, they looked down at a police car as it ramped up into the parking lot, lights on the roof whirling without the siren sounding.

"Help's here."

Fifteen.

She'd gone in to warn everyone about what she'd seen but that all changed when she saw Callie run from the man who'd attacked her. "Callie!" Dashing toward her. "I told you to stay put!"

Grace wasn't mad at her, she wasn't having a go at her. She just wanted to draw attention away from her and let the attacker know that she wasn't alone anymore. That she wasn't his to have.

As she reached the vending machine that had swallowed her change, the door to the locker room exploded behind her. Grace felt a rush of air buffet her forward and a spray of dust cover her. She also heard a rush of water and turned quickly to see what was going on in there. It looked as though the plumbing had erupted.

Her outstretched hands felt Callie's reach for her and Grace took them, barging her way through into the nearest ward. They'd be safer in there away from the tall ugly figure, the burst pipes in the changing room, and snake eggs from the generator shed. "This way!"

After securing the only way in, she led the girl to the back of the old eye infirmary to a set of consultation rooms. They'd be safe back there, away from the main thoroughfare. Once inside, Callie went into overdrive, pushing the bed in front of the door and rifling through the desk for something sharp. Grace rolled up the closed blinds to watch their escape route.

Tiredness clouded Grace's vision, made it tunnel out in front of her. It happened to her a lot as a kid. The room she was in would elongate, making objects suddenly seem unreachable when they were easily within reach or squishy when they were solid. Something similar was happening to her now and Grace feared the world would never right itself, just as she had back then, as a kid.

"Hey?" Callie's quiet voice flipped everything back to normal. "There's something I need to tell you." The worried look in the girl's eyes made Grace smile. It reminded her of her daughter, Jade, when she was worried about nothing.

Shaking her head, she told Callie it didn't matter. Whatever it was, was hardly worse than what was going on all around them. About to tell the girl what she had seen in the generator shed, the dull room suddenly filled with blue and red lights. Spinning around to see a police car arrive loosened the pressure building up inside her. "Help's here."

The two women watched it pull into the carpark and circle around out of sight.

"Do those windows open?"

From the looks of them, they'd been painted shut. There were two which appeared capable of being pushed upwards; Callie grabbed one while Grace went for the other. Together, they crouched and pushed against the tight frame. Neither budged more than an inch or so. Although they were still on the ground floor, the area's hilly landscape meant that they were slightly elevated above the carpark. If they could get out, the drop would be just shy of five feet. While Callie would be fine, Grace would need to dangle before losing her grip to make it down without injuring herself.

To her right, her friend had both hands through the gap between the window and its frame and was heaving it up with a creak, inch by agonizing inch. Progress stopped, though, when a sharp clunk under the sink pulled their attention away. Knocking into her, Callie told Grace, "Get away from the sink."

Leaving the window, Grace was herded back toward the door. More knocking sounds echoed from the sink hole.

"Is this what happened in the changing rooms?"

Callie wasn't listening to her. Still backing away from the sink and windows, one arm shielding her. "We've got to get out of here."

A crash against the door behind them shook the bed frame and spun them both around. The girl screamed. Grace saw why, a jet of water popped the nozzle off the tap clean off. It pinged across the room, ricocheting against the desk and skittering along the floor. Another thump from the other side of the door sent the bed squeaking away from its moorings.

Both women were huddled in the center of the small room, eyeing the opposing dangers. The pipework beneath the sink groaned, the fittings clanking against the wall. With a shudder, the jet of water slowed until only air puffed out. On the other side of the door, all went quiet.

"Have they gone?"

Grace got her phone out, found the torch function and aimed the light at the sink. Something was foaming out of the tap. "What is that?"

Bubbles oozed out, sparkling in the faint light from her phone. She knew what it was when an inch-long wriggling tail emerged, whipping back and forth. "Snakes." Grace gasped out the word.

Callie snatched the phone from her hand. The beam of light shook as the girl aimed it at the sink. "No, no, no, no, no."

A loud thud against the door jerked their

attention. Grace felt her device thrust back into her palm before the girl shot against the bed to keep it from moving any further, pushing it in front of the door. A fleshy lump dropped into the sink, squirming. It was fat, slimy, and ugly. Shivers shuddered up her back on sight. In the glare of light, she saw the sign fixed on the rear wall: *caution hot water*.

Bounding forward, Grace knocked the tap on full before stumbling out of harm's way. The pipes beneath the sink clanged and rattled. Two more bright white slugs plopped from the tap, forced out by a surge of scalding water. The stream almost ripped the metal fixture from its ceramic housing. Plumes of steam rose from the sink, drowning out their squeals.

"Die, just fucking die!" Callie was back next to her, screaming her voice raw at the clouds of steam engulfing the snakes.

At the door, the thrashing got worse. Whoever was out there was dead intent on getting inside.

Callie whirled around, aiming her venom toward the other side of the barricaded door, "You're too late, bitch! Your babies are dead!"

Babies?

Grace wrenched her eyes from the door, across to the gushing sink, scalding water overflowing the basin along with the dead lumps slapping down onto the wet floor.

Those eggs in the generator shed had been laid by something bigger. Whatever had bitten Keith. "What's outside, Callie?" The girl's wild eyes stared through her, unfocused. Gently, Grace took hold of her shoulders and put herself in her line of sight. "Callie, what's on the other side of that door?"

The thrashing and knocking persisted, unabated. The girl continued to stare, breathing hard, seemingly incapable of speech.

"Please, Callie, what kind of snake is it? My friend's been bit and we may need the antidote to the venom."

That's when the girl's eyes locked onto hers and the laughing began. Not soft, humorous laughter but the manic kind of the doomed and deflated. "Snake?" she managed. "There's no snake. Do these things look like snakes to you?" Taking hold of Grace's shoulders and forcing her to look down at the dead lumps which lay scattered across the flooding consultation room floor.

"No." It was true. Those eggs, they didn't look like any snake eggs she'd ever seen. And that thing, worming up from the sewers, she knew they weren't snakes.

"I don't know what the fuck it is." Quieter now, the laughter gone, her arms limp at her sides. Seemingly calmed as the barrage of attacks to the door refused to abate. "But it came from the tanker truck, killed the driver and now it's coming for me."

Sixteen.

No sooner had they spotted the car than they saw him.

"There." Cross was already on the move.

Anderson followed him, dodging around the plastic waiting room chairs after the lanky figure who'd disappeared into the darkened corridor.

"Callie!" A scream, from deep within the hallways.

Anderson recognized the name and woman doing the screaming. But before either of them could get there, an explosion knocked everyone sideways. A cloud of dust and debris cloaked the corridor and the figures that darted in opposite directions through different darkened doorways.

Within the mess, Anderson caught sight of the guy, headed left into a shadowy changing room. She followed him and the sound of water spray, Cross on her heels. A line of grey metal lockers covered one wall and wooden benches along another. Sinks at the other end and an archway into the toilets. The tile floor was slick with a widening pool of running water. It sparkled in the dull moonlight shining down through the skylight.

"That way." Rushing in as the tall man ducked through the archway.

Cross and Anderson spread out. They both knew what the man was capable of. He'd abducted more than one girl, from the looks of his cabin. Had gone for her when Anderson found him lying by the back door and had driven into her partner, almost killing him. If they followed him into a dead end, he'd react like a cornered animal.

"Ready?"

Anderson nodded to Cross.

Slowly, they moved in, their boots sloshing in the bubbling tide of water. She caught a whiff of its stench and realized it was not just fresh tap water but was also wastewater, flowing up from the drains.

Breathing through her mouth, Anderson edged closer to the archway. Her shadow falling across her feet as she moved away from the room's only natural light source. Blinking on beside her, stark in the room, she turned to see Cross had his phone in hand. The beam brought out what was left of the cubicle stalls. Despite the shadowy recesses, there was no one there.

"Where'd he go?"

Cross shook his head. The light in his hand eased down to the gaping, splintered crack in the floor. "Down there. The same way that thing must've got in."

"Well, I'm not going down there," Anderson said, bending at the waist to check beneath the stall doors that were still in place. "What now?"

Turning around on the spot, Cross offered,

"I'll make some calls and get this place surrounded."

It sounded like a plan. Once everyone got there, she could maybe clock off and go home for something to eat, maybe catch up on some sleep. Although, having the place surrounded brought to mind Waco and bloodshed. But only for a moment. That kind of thing never happened in the UK.

"What's going on here?" A deep masculine voice cut through Anderson's thoughts. Cross' phone light swung up and caught a hospital security guard standing in the open doorway, water lapping at his feet.

The two suits retrieved their warrant cards and flashed them at him. "Detectives Anderson and Cross, we've tracked a man wanted for questioning to this hospital."

The security guard inched closer, squinting at their identification.

"Any ideas how we turn this water off?"

The guard nodded and splashed over to the sinks. "Think there's a valve somewhere under here."

The sound of rushing water slowed and then

stopped, though the bubbling of waste sewer water continued. There was no valve to stop that.

"What can I do to help?"

Anderson smiled and left her partner to talk strategy while she went back out into the corridor. A few people were milling around; hospital staff and patients who had ventured out of the main waiting area with nothing better to do than see what all the fuss was about.

Next to the vending machine, a set of locked double doors caught her attention. "What's through there?" she asked a porter. When they'd gone rushing into the hallway, she remembered hearing someone shout 'Callie!' and saw figures disappearing in that direction. It had to be the girl and the nurse.

"The old eye infirmary."

"Can you get these doors open?" Flashing her warrant card which was still clutched in her hand.

The man shook his head. "It's locked from the other side. But we can get in from around the back."

Cross and the security guard stepped out into the hall.

"I'm going to check on Callie and the

nurse."

Cross nodded. "Meet back in the waiting room?"

Anderson tipped her head and followed the porter. As she reached the main desk, she heard Cross ask if someone could get the power back on. She didn't catch the reply.

"You here because of that tanker driver?"

News travelled fast. "Yeah, we found the killer's car parked outside." It wasn't strictly true, though they knew he was a killer.

"I can ask Vern to get it towed." A nod back at the security guard followed by a cheeky smile from the porter.

It wasn't such a bad idea. Forensics would want to look at it anyway and it wouldn't hurt to deprive the attacker of a getaway car. "You ever think of being a cop?"

A scream ripped through the gloom. It was so loud and grating that she couldn't decipher the direction it came from. It seemed to echo from all corners, all around them.

"Hold him down!" A yell as the scream was still petering out. It came from behind reception, where the A and E cubicles were.

Anderson broke into a run. Maybe Callie's attacker had gotten out and around the back? He wouldn't get away this time. Crashing against the desk, her hip taking most of the impact, it threatened to drop her again. The porter was right there with her. She bumped into him instead of falling. It got her around the corner and closer to the growling voice.

"Hold him still…Jesus, what is that?"

Anderson thought she knew.

A crowd of nurses and paramedics had circled the commotion. Even in the twilight hue, she could see the blood sparkle. See it as loud and bright as the screams bouncing off the walls. On autopilot, she pushed her way through into the scrum of people. Holding down a man spewing bloody worms, in his fifties with a gash on his right leg while a nurse was doubled over, choking on the same wiggling bloody forms. It wasn't the same man. But he had the same things inside him. Crawling, twisting, squirming across the floor.

"Get back!" Anderson pushed the people away from those things. At her feet, she saw them. And her boot stamp down, over and over, crushing them. Hearing their tinny squeaks.

"Damn it!" One of the male nurses next to her. Staring at the bite mark on his exposed forearm. At the flapping worms burrowing down into and under his flesh.

The other man securing the injured party, when he saw what was happening, let him go. Mouth open silent. He just backed away. As they all were doing.

The man with the worms spiraling from his bloody mouth, that seeping wound on his leg. He spun; eyes fixed on Anderson. Blank, black eyes staring into hers. A grin spreading across his face. Skin slick and moving with those things beneath his flesh.

"Help me!" the nurse screamed. "Get them out of me!"

Seventeen.

Holding back the bed, as the door buckled. Behind her, Grace had shut off the water. Those things coming up through the pipes were all dead.

"Help me!" Braced against the bed, screaming over her shoulder. "They're coming in!"

Callie couldn't hold them back on her own. "Grace? Please!" Why was she standing there, doing nothing?

As the bed rocked, Callie twisted to see. The nurse's face, pale and slack, stared past her. Callie followed her gaze to the floor beneath the bed. When she saw them, she jumped away. Letting the bed rock back and roll away from the door. Those things. They were coming in through a gap. She felt Grace haul her back out of harm's way.

"Grab that chair."

Tearing her gaze from the worms squirming across the floor, Callie latched onto the office chair. Grace let her go and stepped back. The window in clear view. With a roar, she hefted that chair over her shoulder and lunged it at the window. The glass exploded, some of it inside, but not all of it left the frame. With a screech, she wanged the chair again, this time all the glass fell clear.

"Come on!"

As Grace turned to the window, Callie flung the office chair at the bed and creatures scurrying across the floor. She took the outstretched hand and followed her friend to the window.

There was a white doctors coat on a hook next to one of the filing cabinets; Callie swiped it down and laid it over the bottom of the window frame and shards of glass still poking up.

"You first."

Callie nodded and stuck her head out through the frame. There was a bit of a drop but nothing compared to what those things coming for her could do. Legs dangling over the edge, Callie twisted herself around, both hands clutching tight. She pushed herself off and let herself drop and roll. The landing jarred her.

She looked up, slightly breathless; Grace came out next. Callie wasn't sure whether to try and catch her or stand aside and give her some space.

The nurse didn't wait, she just dropped, the wind visibly knocked out with a whomp as she hit the uneven ground. Above them, in the consultation room, they heard the door burst open with a crash.

"Come on." Callie helping up her friend and, together, they stumbled back toward the nurse's car.

Eighteen.

Grace couldn't help looking backward. Since leaving her husband, constantly looking forward was getting harder for her to do. At the open window, she saw the figure. If he jumped down, she wouldn't be able to get away. Bent over, the fall had knocked the air out of her. Her gasps were hard and hurt her chest. That and the sharp pain in her leg was slowing Callie down. Fumbling with her free hand for her car keys, she thrust them toward the girl and told her to get to the car.

The girl shook her head. "I'm not going anywhere without you."

Grace almost fell to her knees, tears peppering her eyes. Together, they rounded the corner, Grace glancing back to check whether the man was still coming. He was gone from the window and nowhere in sight. If he went back the way he'd come, they'd easily out-move him. Up ahead, her car was in sight. But was blocked in by a police car, lights flashing, sirens silent.

"No!"

Callie stopped to check on her. Grace pointed over toward the car. "We're blocked in."

But her friend was smiling. "The police are here."

Officers were standing next to the generator shed, all lit up in the police car's main beam. As it twigged, the hospital building suddenly lit up. The power was back on.

"Get away from there!" Grace screamed her warning.

Heads turning, detective Cross and another man ducked out through the doorway and clocked them. Quickening his step, Cross pulled out his phone and stuck it to his ear. They made it to the car before he reached them.

"Stay put, I'll be right there," into the phone before he stuffed it back into his pocket. "Get them in the car." Pointing to a uniformed officer who turned and opened a rear door for Grace and Callie.

"Those things are in the generator shed; did you see them?" Grace pausing at the open door.

Cross shook his head. "You're safe now, stay in the car, okay?"

She helped Callie inside then shuffled in after her friend. As the door was closed, they watched Cross meet back up with the man—who she now recognized as Vern, one of the security guards—and head back inside the main building. She didn't want to just sit there and wait but then, where else was safer than the back of a police car, surrounded by police officers?

"You okay?" Looking over at Callie and realizing she was asking stupid questions, again.

A smile. "I need to pee."

That made them both chuckle. At least this car didn't smell as bad as the last one. Between the seat back, Grace watched the uniformed officers milling around outside. Two stood in front of the open doorway to the generator shed. She slapped her palms against the glass of the side window to get their attention.

"It's okay, I can hold it." Callie nudged her.

"I didn't tell you about the eggs."

Her friend's smile fell.

And that's when the yelling started.

Nineteen.

Reaching over to the porter, Anderson asked him, "We need somewhere to quarantine them—a room with a lock on the door."

The porter eyed the nurses.

"You're not locking me up in the same room as him." The male nurse, breathing hard, still clutching onto his bitten, infected forearm.

"There's a couple of doctor's rooms through there."

That would do. "Okay, give me a hand with him." Nodding at the man who was being newly restrained by two paramedics.

Still struggling and grinning, the skin warbling on his face, he was hauled up and manhandled across the floor.

She turned to the two injured nurses.

"Follow me."

The male nurse slowly shook his head. The female nurse, she was still bent double, puking out those things in swirls of stringy, blood speckled bile.

With a flash overhead, the lights blazed, the power humming back online. Watching as the man was walked out of sight by the porter, Anderson reached for her phone to call Cross. She kept the two nurses in view, a growing pool of glistening blood spreading across the ground. Those fat, pale worms writhing and flopping in the puddle of ooze.

Cross answered.

"We've got a situation, here."

She heard him breath out, "Stay put, I'll be right there."

In her face, the male nurse hovered, pointing down at his colleague retching. "We need to get Gwen some help."

Anderson kept her mouth shut.

"And that bloke you had carted off, he's a friend of ours. Something bit him; he's not a bad guy."

"He bit you." Pointing down at the man's forearm, then across at the female nurse. "I have no idea what he did to her; he needs to be quarantined before he bites or does anything to anyone else."

A fresh scream ripped apart the room.

"Stay here," she told him, "please," then followed the noise from the back of the hospital.

Footsteps pounded behind her. "Lucy!" It was Cross and the security guard, Vern.

Slowing down but not stopping, she told him they had another one. "He bit two nurses."

"He the maintenance man?"

Vern and Cross locked eyes. "His name's Keith."

The groans were getting louder, the closer they got. Anderson could see the rooms. And the porter, rushing out from one of them. "'He bit someone else." Behind him, the sound of glass shattering spun him around.

Cross and Vern pushed past. Anderson followed. There was blood everywhere. All over a paramedic writhing on the ground. Anderson spotted the other paramedic who she'd sent to haul Keith back there. He was just stood in place, hands on his head, gazing out of the broken window.

"Where'd he go?" Cross asked him.

Though it was pretty obvious. Spots of sparkling blood trailed across the floor and out through the shattered window.

"Damn it!" Cross had his phone out. "Yeah, Jerry, I need you at the back of A and E. He's attacked three nurses."

Anderson turned to the porter. "Any other nurses in?"

The man shook his head. "Not until shift change at six."

She checked her watch. It wasn't even four yet.

"Jerry! What's going on?" Cross shouting into his phone.

"Grace is out in the car. Something's wrong." Cross had coaxed the paramedic out. To him, he asked, "Can you get on the phone and call in some help?"

The paramedic was in shock, but he nodded all the same.

Then Cross was gone, Vern at his heels.

"What about him?" The porter pointed down at the paramedic on the ground, now seemingly unconscious in one of the doorways.

"We can't do anything without more help."

Twenty.

"Get them off me! Get them off me!"

Hard as she tried, Callie couldn't get the doors open. Grace's palms thudded against the glass as her friend screamed at them to let her out.

Between the seat backs, caught in the glare of the headlight beams, they watched those things besiege the officers. It happened slowly, at first. The officer closest to the generator shed, Callie saw him kick at something on the ground. A moment or so later, the same man started jiggling his right leg like it had gone to sleep. After that, they just swarmed him. All of them.

He was on the ground, now, rolling around screaming for his colleagues to get them off him. But there were too many of them and they were fast. Nothing like that fat glob that she first saw slide down the tanker truck cab windscreen and squirm off into the night. Those little baby worms moved like grass snakes. And they were on all of them, all three officers' screams drowned out by Grace's frantic yelling next to her.

Up front, the police radio crackled to life. Grace stopped pounding at the window. Callie caught her eye, but the look was only fleeting. Her friend was over the front seats, legs kicking in the air, arms reaching for the radio.

"Help us, help us, please!"

In response, static crackled out.

Grace tried again. But there was nothing of any sense coming back. Callie's fingers sunk into the seat. They'd tried the rear doors but not the front.

"Try the door."

Grace dropped the radio, scrambled around—pulling her legs down so that she was sitting up—and popped the handle. But, just like the radio, nothing happened. "It's locked!" Spinning around, wide eyes staring across at her.

"Try the other one."

Jumping across to the passenger side, the nurse wrenched the handle in front of Callie. That, too, wouldn't budge.

Outside, all was quiet. There were no more

screams. No more shouting to get those things off them. No more of anything.

"What we gonna do?"

Callie didn't know. Just like she didn't know what that sound was. It was like a rustling, clanking noise, coming up from under the engine block.

"What *is* that?" Grace faced front, head angled under the dash. Whatever it was, was getting louder, closer.

"Grace, get in the back." Callie said the words so calmly, it was like it never happened. Maybe, she just thought them in her own head? So, she said them again, louder his time. "Grace, get in the back." Her hands were on her shoulders. Soft at first, then firm, squeezing so hard she could feel bone. Callie was gripping her friend so tightly, it must have hurt.

Grace squealed, jerking back; practically threw herself between the front seats to get away. "They're coming, they're coming!"

Callie didn't have to ask. As they poked their heads out through the vents, she knew what was coming and what would happen next.

Twenty-one.

Taking Callie's hand, Grace scrambled over the front seats and collapsed against her friend who had started clawing at the rear headrests.

"Help me get these seats down."

There was another out.

Twisting around to check on those things, their pale white bodies continued to squirm through the air vents before dropping down and disappearing into the dark footwells. There wasn't much time. Those things were growing bigger and quicker. She'd seen them move and take down three police officers in a matter of minutes out in the open. Trapped inside a medium sized family hatchback, it wouldn't take them long to overpower two skinny, sleep-deprived women.

"Get your side."

Grace pulled her focus away from the front of the car and zeroed in on what her friend was doing. A latch next to the headrest released the back seat so that it could fold down. Grace found hers and wrenched that side free. Together they hopped over it as it dropped, opening up the rear boot space. No sooner was it down, than Callie was in there, ducking under the parcel shelf which was still fixed in place. Grace crawled down there with her, blinking her eyes against the grainy darkness.

"Can you get it open?" Desperation in every word.

The girl palmed the door, but it wouldn't budge. "There's not enough light to see down here."

The nurse shuffled back and shouldered the parcel shelf upward, hoping to dislodge it. It gave after three cracks, raising in the center like a steeple. The girl came up and pounded on the now flimsy board until it could be pulled free. Grace flung it into the front of the car, watching for the incoming invaders.

More pounding from her friend brought her back to the task at hand, whatever she was doing wasn't working. Pulling her feet under her, she flipped onto her back and tucked her knees into her chest. "Move aside."

Callie eyed her and shifted back.

Kicking out, Grace gave it her all. The impact of her soles against the rear windscreen shocked up through, into her knees which were already throbbing. All that came back was a dull thud.

Next to her, Callie braced to join her. "After three."

Grace nodded and counted down with her, lashing out at the glass as one. A louder thud that time, a hairline fracture appearing

"Again."

The women counted to three and kicked out hard. A sharp pain buzzing in Grace's right knee at the moment of impact. A crack followed the thud.

"One more should do it."

On two, Grace felt something in her hair and screamed. She was up, panic flinging her hands to her head, knocking away the worms she could feel weighing down her locks.

"Hold still." Her friend, as calm as she was when they'd first spotted them coming in through the car's heating system.

Squeezing shut her eyes, Grace did as she was told and kept herself still. Rough hands patted her hair, shoulders and back. She could hear those things plop onto the car's upholstery. A crash from the front opened her eyes as they both screamed out. Through the windscreen, stark in the headlights, stood Detective Cross and Vern the security guard, wielding a fire extinguisher apiece.

They were saved.

Hefting it behind them, Cross and Vern brought them down again at the lower far corners of the glass. The windscreen bucked, splintering, with cracks travelling up into the center. After hitting it again, the glass webbed. With an explosive roar, Cross kept it up until they could no longer see out and the glass fell in on itself.

"Shut your eyes."

The last thing Grace saw were the two men unclasping their hoses and pointing them down into the car. After that, with her eyes squeezed tight, she heard the pressure release valves hiss and felt the air around them go horribly cold. Like the noise she heard back in the generator shed, those things squealed as they were doused in foam. They were so loud, it drowned out the sound of the spray.

"Take my hand!" Cross shouting to be heard above everything.

Grace ripped open her eyes and saw two sets of hands reaching in to pull them free. The inside of the car now buried in white foam.

The nurse took Cross' hands and kicked off from the backseat as Callie latched onto Vern's. Both of them were pulled up and out through the open front of the car.

Once out, Cross stopped her automatic urge run. "Grace, we need your help inside."

Twenty-two.

With Cross gone and the paramedic on the phone, Anderson and the porter went to check on the two injured nurses they'd left behind. On their way back around, her phone went off. Checking the call ID, it was Matt Hague, one of their Detective Constables: "What you got for me?"

"Just sent you the preliminary postmortem

for the truck driver."

Her phone buzzed against her ear at the email notification.

"Interesting reading."

She didn't have time to read it now, they were in the middle of a shit storm. "Give me the short version."

"Okay, cause of death is still undetermined."

Anderson shook her head as the main desk came into view. She supposed death by worm wasn't on the list of available options.

"This is not in the report, but the Doc is leaning towards some kind of animal attack, though nothing she's seen before." Matt's voice in her ear trailed off once she got to where she was going.

On the floor, Gwen was dead. The nurse was sprawled in a pool of sparkling blood. Whirling around, the male nurse was nowhere to be seen. In her ear, the DC continued talking: "If she were to hazard a guess, the closest thing in nature would be a hookworm."

Other than the small worms she stamped on earlier, those too were gone. She turned to the porter, who was just staring down at the mess. She told him, "Go check the waiting area."

After a blink, he nodded and left.

"The Doc showed me a photo, it's all teeth—pretty gruesome looking thing. But get this, it's the kind of worm your typical domesticated pet might get. These things are the size and length of a string of spaghetti."

Staring down at what was left of those things, they were much bigger than that but not nearly as long. These were shorter but still had teeth.

"To cause the kind of injuries documented on the truck driver, this thing would have to be bigger than any worm—bigger than a fully grown Anaconda!"

Her head was flooded with those images from the cab's dashcam: the gaping hole it had left in the nurses changing rooms and the babies that had burrowed into several innocent people.

"The Doc, she estimated it to be about the size of a meaty human thigh but approximately six to ten feet in length."

Based on what had been captured on the

dashcam, the Doc wasn't far off. "It's big." Anderson had to get it out, had to tell someone else about what she'd seen. "But that's not the worst of it."

A pause in her ear. "Wait, you've seen it?" Barely a static whisper.

"Detective?" The porter's voice calling out to her from the other side of the main desk. The tone of urgency prickled all down along her back.

Moving away from the body and around to the main waiting area, what greeted her was more carnage. On the floor, sprawled across the plastic chairs. Piled up and left in individual clumps. It registered in flashes. Everyone was dead.

"How're things there?"

Fucked was how things were but the words wouldn't come.

"I couldn't get hold of Cross, is he with you?"

Cross…

Anderson spun around to the corridor he'd dashed down earlier to get the nurse. "He wasn't answering his phone?" Leaving the dumbstruck porter, his eyes down at the bodies, she headed back. As long as she'd known Cross, that phone of his never went unanswered.

"Just rang out. Tried him, like, four or five times before I rang you. Wait, he's coming back…" Matt's voice dropped an octave or two in her ear. "This guy's strange."

That stopped her. "Strange how? Where are you?"

"Waste treatment plant." Like it was obvious. "Cross asked me to check out the place, but the security guard here…I don't know."

It came to her. When they were in the back of the ambulance, she remembered Cross on the phone. He'd sent him there to check if there were any more of those things where the tanker driver had last done a pick-up.

"Hey Matt, what's so strange about him?" She didn't like the way he was talking. Matt Hague had joined their department a couple of years back and wasn't the kind of bloke that spooked easily. Whenever they'd been assigned together, he was one of the DCs she knew she could count on to have her back. A street brawl that had escalated came to the forefront of her mind. He'd held his own that night until back up had arrived.

A static exhale in her ear. In a whisper, he told her, "Just this weird grin he's got plastered across is face…he's got this kinda blank stare, the man doesn't say much. And his skin…"

In her head was the man who started all this off. The one who took Callie. The one she found on the kitchen floor of the cabin with those things swarming around under his face. Where there was a big one, the little ones would be close by. "What about his skin?" Even Anderson was whispering now.

A nervous laugh, all static, it tickled her ear. "Just…he's got these bulges in his skin, like there's something under there."

A crash along the corridor brought her out of the conversation and back into the hospital. It got Anderson moving again. Cross was in trouble. In her phone, she told Matt, "Get away from him, he's got those hookworms in him."

"Huh?" Followed by a clump on the other end of the phone. Then a heavy clatter. It sounded to her like Matt had dropped his handset.

"Matt! Hey, Matt?" Stopping in the doorway. But all that she heard was dead air for a second before the line dropped out.

From her phone, her eyes went up to the hallway. And the lanky figure stalking there. It was him. He was facing away from her, but it was definitely him. Beyond him, a crowd rushed in. Cross, Vern, Callie, and Grace.

When she saw them, Anderson let out a breath she hadn't realized was being held in and moved forward. He was okay. They were all okay.

From a side door, two other figures emerged from the shadows of the nurses' changing room. The male nurse and maintenance guy. Both of them turned on her. Anderson backed up, slowly, putting distance between them. Ahead, Cross paused, holding the girls back behind his outstretched arms.

A crash caught Anderson's eye; drew everyone's attention. Behind Cross, through the same door he'd just burst through, more were coming.

Twenty-three.

"Shit. Oh, shit, oh shit!"

Rustling behind the detective, Callie's eyes were everywhere. They were trapped. She held tight onto Grace's hand.

"Stay close, okay?" Cross had them. He wouldn't let anything happen to them. The fire extinguishers might be empty and gone but she knew they'd be okay. Next to Callie, Grace shifted, still muttering to herself. In the narrow space, like her, they were all looking for a way out.

Away from the attacker, over by the vending machines, just standing there watching them. With him, two others. Waiting. Cross had them pushed back against the wall. To her right, the officers from outside, with those things inside them, they all stood in the doorway, also waiting. Watching.

Feeling a slight pull on her left hand, Grace,

her eyes wide, jerked her head. Callie looked to where her friend was nodding, eyes climbing higher to the elevator sign hanging down from the ceiling. Locking stares, Callie nodded fast. She heard the nurse's hand palm the wall.

Cross heard it, too. She followed his head and eyes to the wall, then up to the ceiling sign. Grace's slapping stopped. Through the wall, they all heard the soft clunk and whir of the lift motor kicking in. Blue LED numbers flashed from 03 down to 02, the directional arrow showing the way.

Checking his surroundings, Cross moved them closer to the lift doors, shuffling them ever so slowly so as not to draw anyone else's attention. Away from the officers stationed in the doorway—his former colleagues.

Callie checked. 01. Almost there. Gripping tightly to the nurse's hand, she willed the creatures not to move. Although she could see the potential shift in them, in their blank stares, those spreading grins, those things moving around beneath their skin. Did they know what they were doing, that they'd called the lift?

Before the stainless-steel elevator doors, they waited. At once they saw and heard its arrival. 00, and a ting that sounded much louder that it should have.

Callie's eyes went to the three officers in the doorway. They were all hunkered down low, as if they were about to pounce or rush them. Over at the other end of the long corridor, the guy from the cabin and his two friends, they were all standing up straight backed. The other detective, she was back there, wanting to help but powerless to do anything but wait for a window. Now the lift was there, Callie saw her dash from the doorway and disappear.

A monstrous rumbling overhead. It both felt and sounded like the ceiling was coming down. Dirty off-white, square ceiling tiles above them cracked and splintered. The strip light fixtures in between rattled then blinked out, plunging them back into a chasm of darkness.

All four of them, backs against the lift doors, waiting for them to part, when a whole chuck of ceiling crashed to their feet. Amongst the falling debris, a shape dropped, narrowly missing Cross.

"Doors opening."

The automated voice causing Callie to

flinch. She felt her arm being pulled and let the tide of movement take her where she needed to go.

They bunched into the long, brightly lit lift car. Out in the dark hallway, in the shocking stillness, dust in the air, she saw what had burrowed down into the corridor.

"Get the doors!" Cross' voice urgent as Grace's hand punched at the panel of buttons opposite.

That thing, almost grey in color—its whole body now saturated in grime and dirt—reared up, mouth full of teeth and red pulsing eyes, lunged for them.

"Doors closing."

Hitting the back of the lift, her head connecting with the mirror. Cross made sure he was the one in harm's way.

It was much bigger, now. A mutation. That thing she'd watched emerge from beneath the changing room floor had grown up fast. It was now the size and shape of an adult seal. Those officers stationed in the doorway, they were out of sight but in no way out of mind. With their mother here, Callie just knew they would hold their ground. Would not come any closer.

Would not interfere. Whatever that was, it was not their moment, and they knew to stay out of the way.

The lift doors began sliding shut. To Callie, it took forever but was probably no slower than usual. The worm rose up like a Cobra. As the doors were coming together, she had a thought they were safe. That it wouldn't strike. That thing she'd seen squirm away from the tanker truck cab was not quick enough to get to them now.

She was wrong.

In a blink, it was no longer there in the corridor. In the time it took Callie's eyes to focus, that thing had darted forward. It crashed against the closing lift doors, stopping their seamless meeting in the middle.

To her left, Grace hammered at the panel of buttons. The doors juddered. Its face loomed up high, level with their stomachs. Vern reacted first, aiming a steel-capped boot to its head. The worm reeled, squealing out. Callie covered her ears with both hands, falling back into the corner. Two more kicks to the face drove the worm out. The nurse jabbed the button, closing the doors. Ting. "Doors closing."

That thing wasn't giving up. It wriggled into the doors, stopping them, mangling them inward. A well-timed boot from Vern wedged the thing against the door. A clatter as one of the door sensors came unstuck and hit the floor.

"Come on!" Grace didn't quit her pummeling at the panel.

Cross got in there, too. A heel to the creature's face, snapped its head back. The doors slid closed a third time.

Slam. It came again. This time, both men were on it. Their feet stamping it. Another clatter as a second sensor came dislodged. Grace, as ever, attacking the buttons. Callie watched the doors not moving.

"Going down." That automated voice filled her with a wave of sheer calm.

The floor beneath her shifted; they were going down. The two men backed up from the opening as a brick wall and breeze blocks appeared through the broken doors. In a breath, the worm came again. Its face snarling, teeth missing, sparkling shiny blood flying and caking its body.

Twenty-four.

When the whole lift car jerked them down, Grace fell back away from the panel of buttons she'd been pounding. Her index finger stung from jabbing at the door button. With a glance, she realized the nail had split, half of it gone and replaced with blood.

In that second, the monster came at them, again. Slouching down onto the floor next to Callie, she took her friend's hand as they looked on. Its head was through the opening, looming over Cross and Vern who had started backing away.

"Come on." Cross eyed the panel of buttons as though they could speed up their descent.

There was a crunch, a squeal of tension from above before the noise from that thing joined it. It was sickening to watch. Grace wanted to rise, then jump up and down on the floor so that the lift would decapitate the creature quicker.

Those fiery red eyes bulged as the car eased down and the gap became narrower. A whirring sound moaned louder, flinging them up and then the smooth motion resumed. The worm's massive head exploded, a sparkling shower of blood and gore splashing the walls before it flopped, bounced face-first to the floor, writhing, squealing, even though it was now half the worm it used to be.

"Fuck," Vern volleyed it with a toe, and it upended, slapping the left door then righted itself.

"It's still alive! How?"

With a grimace on his face, Vern told her, "Worms don't die that way."

Her mind flashed back to being a kid, watching her big brother snap an earthworm with a spade and seeing both halves keep on wriggling.

They hadn't escaped it. Now there were two of them.

"Basement level." That automated voice announced their arrival below the hospital.

"Cross?" Through the half open doors, Anderson came into view.

"Watch out, it's not dead," Cross said as he and the security guard leant against a door each and shouldered them apart.

Squirming in its own blood and bile, those red eyes rolling around, broken teeth gnashing up at them, Grace couldn't look away.

"Everyone out." Anderson urging them up. To the porter—Alan, she thought it was—she asked him, "Is there a back way out of here?"

Looking pale and nauseous, he blinked and pointed toward the fire doors. "Through there."

The way out was right across from where her car was parked. That got her on her feet until she remembered the ex-police officers stationed by the incinerator room. "We can't go that way."

Cross turned to her, eyebrows raised.

"Those men by the back door."

He left the group, heading off along the corridor. Anderson followed him, "What's the plan?"

Grace helped Callie to her feet then inched out, giving what was left of the creature a wide berth. Vern helped them cross the threshold. Along the hall, the detectives came with fire extinguishers. Seeing them made Grace smile.

"You ready?" Cross saw her smile and matched it.

"Not yet." Behind them, Callie nodded down at the wiggling form. "Douse it."

Anderson didn't get it, but Cross caught on. Shifting around in the doorway, he unclasped the nozzle. With a blast of cold foam, he sprayed the thing until it stopped shrieking and bubbles rose up from its mangled body.

"All good?" Smiling over at Callie.

Grace took her friend's arm in hers and led her away. They were both unsteady on their feet, which was no surprise given what they'd been through tonight. When she got home, Grace was going to sleep the entire weekend. If Callie wanted company, her friend could have her daughter's bed. They'd order take aways and watch terrible movies until it was time to pick her daughter up from her dads on Sunday night.

Outside, dawn was rising. The sun inked the sky in wild pink and blues. Grace wanted to run to her car but held back. Before she could go anywhere, they still had to move the police car blocking her in.

"Hey Vern, you want to escort the ladies to

their car?" Cross pointed it out to him.

"Where are you two going?" Callie's question stopped everyone.

Twenty-five.

With much of the ceiling gone, Cross used his phone to light up the floor. Amongst the debris, there was no sign of the worm's other half.

Like the waiting area, the corridor outside the elevator was a mess of bodies. Everybody was dead.

Anderson had tiptoed over sprawled legs, arms, and body parts to reach the vending machines where two more bodies lay stale and hollowed out.

"They all have holes in them."

Anderson looked up at her partner's statement. She watched him step gingerly over the crime scene to meet her.

"When we split that thing in two, I think all the little babies—whatever they are—went to it."

It made sense. As much as any of this could. "So where is it?"

Cross replied with a shrug.

There was no sign of anything in what was left of the flooded changing room or in the main waiting area. "I'm not going back down into the basement, again."

They walked outside where the sound of approaching sirens grew louder. When the lift had descended, Anderson went for the stairs and called their boss in. Pushing through the fire doors and stepping out onto the carpark, it looked like he had sent everyone.

Across from them, the two women were sat in their car. Vern was perched on the bonnet of the police car with the missing windscreen which had been moved aside. They stepped over to the overwrought women.

"You two take care of each other."

Callie and Grace smiled up at her. "You too."

With that, the car pulled away.

A splash registered off to the right and Anderson followed the sound. Beyond the hospital building lay a stretch of canal. A circle of ripples radiated out from the murky water, bubbles popping on the surface.

A crunch of gravel and Cross was beside her. "There they go."

They'd have to get in touch with British Waterways and have them close off the canal. Otherwise some fisherman might get bit and go ape. The thought gave her a headache.

"Detectives." Strolling across the carpark was their boss. "Someone wanna fill me in on why I'm out here before the sun's even up?"

———

It was after noon by the time Anderson got home. She stepped over the post and pushed the front door closed behind her. In the stillness, her ears rang and head throbbed. She was hungry, tired, and exhausted. She'd left Cross at the station and drove home in a daze. He told her to get some sleep and would call her later. Her phone went on silent in the kitchen, where she paused for a moment, contemplating eating something.

Tiredness and the pull of her bed took over.

Anderson dropped onto her unmade bed, fully clothed, thinking. Detective Constable

Matt Hague was okay. He'd managed to get away from the security guard at the waste treatment plant. His phone needed a new screen but, like the man himself, it could be fixed. The treatment plant had been secured and cordoned off. People in hazmat suits were surveying and cataloging the scene.

The hospital would probably never fully reopen again. It had been cited for closure soon, anyway, so the Trust would simply bring that forward and reassign the remaining staff like Grace Wan to a nearby post. She'd checked in on her and both women had made it back to her house safely. She smiled at the thought of those two and the link they'd forged.

Although Anderson had changed at the station, she still felt like a shower would be a good move. But, like the thought of coffee or food, it could wait until she'd got her head down for a bit. Since she'd joined the force, Anderson needed the TV to sleep. Nothing in particular, just a low background noise — people talking, monotony — to quell the murk in her own head. Twenty-four-hour news stations always worked best.

Kicking off her boots, she thumbed the

remote, crawled under the covers and closed her eyes; willing sleep to come. Talking heads murmured from the speakers; the usual politics of the day Anderson grew weary with, followed by commercials for stuff she didn't need.

The last thought she had before drifting off, concerned the cabin and the man who owned it. Though the abductor had taken Callie and countless others there, it was not his place. It belonged to a former director of the waste treatment plant. Techs had found what was left of his body crammed into the antique looking wardrobe when they'd pried it open. The images had pinged up on Cross' laptop, but Anderson couldn't look at them. When they checked for a next of kin, Callie's abductor popped up. Both brothers were dead. Their bodies and all the others on the ground had been transferred to the morgue. It would keep the doc busy for a while.

As she drifted off into a fractured, dreamless sleep, her phone vibrated on the kitchen counter. With less than ten percent battery remaining, it didn't ring for long.

From across the room, images flickered over Anderson's sleeping form. The low voices that carried with it, spoke of worm sightings in high-rise office buildings and staff panic; sewage water seeping up through cracks in the pavement flooding communities; multi-vehicle pileups along busy carriageways during rush-hour, road rage between stranded commuters; the evacuation of shopping malls. Police were cordoning off huge areas to the public. Social media was in a panic. And no-one from the Government was available for comment.

Acknowledgements.

The release of this book has a nice full-circle moment to it. Back in 1997, aged 17, I got my first short story acceptance. *Desert Expeditions* was a brooding creature feature about a lonely man who trapped exotic pets in the desert and sold them to unscrupulous collectors. No spoilers, but it didn't end well. My third release harks back to that subject matter and the kind of fast-paced horror I loved to read as a teen.

Immeasurable thanks go out to Eddie Generous, purveyor of all things unnerving, for taking a chance on this weird little novella that had been rejected eight times before landing in his inbox. He dug it and I'm eternally grateful. His patience in Americanizing the script and editing my choppy paragraphs into something readable with good humour is nothing short of God-like. And the cover. In a time where AI covers are rampant, there was never any danger of falling foul of that or having to ask for a no AI clause it to be added into the contract as

Unnerving stands against that. His work on the cover was nothing short of remarkable.

Sincere thanks are also due to the writers who agreed to take time out of their schedules to blurb this book. Your kind words mean everything.

My writer mates in cyberspace—Adam Hulse, Paul John Lyon, Radar De Board, Andrew 'the pen' Roberts, Rachael L Tilly, Mark Towse, Rowan Hill, Carol Coney, Ben, Sarah Jane Huntington, Coy Hall, Cherie Mitchell, Craig Wallwork, Set Sharp, Jon Tom and Dave from the Failing Writers Podcast—thanks for your support and encouragement. Without you, I would have given up long ago.

And no acknowledgement page would be complete without bowing down to my favourite girl. I don't know anyone else who can only sleep with a true crime doc playing in the background, loves watching the same TV shows as me and still puts up with my whingeing. Every night is a date night for me.

And finally, Chunkas Malunkas. Reading you bedtime stories is probably my favourite part of the day. Oh, the places we've been.

www.ingramcontent.com/pod-product-compliance
Ingram Content Group UK Ltd.
Pitfield, Milton Keynes, MK11 3LW, UK
UKHW021503240125

4283UKWH00040B/416

9 781998 763672